The Right Side of the River

The Right Side of the River

Romance, Rage, and Wonder

ROGER PINCKNEY

Wyrick & Company
Charleston

*For all the people of Daufuskie, for your love and grit
and fierce independence. But especially for
Miss Susan, who put me up to much of this.*

Published by Wyrick & Company
Post Office Box 89
Charleston, S.C. 29402

Printed in the United States of America

Library of Congress Cataloging-In-Publication Data

Contents

Foreword

by Bo Bryan

The stories collected in this volume are all true. Roger Pinckney is a journalist. Daufuskie Island is a real place. Some of the names have been changed out of respect or affection, others because the actual people are dangerous, not to be antagonized by frivolous accuracy. In some instances, the dangerous are wealthy individuals, who would use the libel laws to stifle publication of the underlying themes these stories contain; they would lose in court, because in front of a jury, the truth is its own defense. Others have been ascribed aliases, who are physically threatening, lawless by nature and live on Daufuskie because, as a general rule, it takes the sheriff about an hour and a half to get here by boat, and, most often, the nefarious as well as the innocent receive fair warning by obscure means.

This is not to say Daufuskie is a violent place. On the contrary, it is not usually necessary to lock your doors at night, nor to worry too much if your children don't get home before sundown. Daufuskie is a loosely interwoven community of fractious groups, like America itself, fraught with desires and cross purposes, but just about all of us love the kids. The resident population is supposed to be about 125, though I've only seen about half that number at any given time, in one spot.

Existing domiciles range in architecture from multimillion

dollar "smart" houses to tar paper shacks. Economic bigotry, in some quarters, is rampant, mainly evident along the frontiers of one or two resort "plantations," where guard shacks have been installed. As everywhere, bigotry and racism are matters of individual ignorance. Generally, the people try to get along; behind closed doors, we mainly disagree over love and money; in public we fight over land.

Oddly enough, most of the trees on Daufuskie are still standing. There are loblolly pines a hundred feet tall, vast live oaks and dwarf palmettos growing in shady fields hidden from even the dirt roads; some of the stoutest magnolia trees I've ever seen grow in my front yard.

The woods are full of deer and birds and ticks and flies and poisonous snakes and, now and then, a bull alligator. There's also a four mile stretch of white sand beach, perhaps a future shooting location for the *Sports Illustrated* swimsuit issue. Super models notwithstanding, last July the Fourth at one o'clock in the afternoon, I counted, along the entire length of Daufuskie, all of twenty odd sunbathers, perhaps half that many dogs, one antique fire engine (driven by an infamous potato cannonier) six or eight seemingly abandoned golf carts and a pickup truck, hauling among other things, a woman with customized contact lenses which made her eyes look like those of a blue tiger.

As yet, the homesteaders and tourists have not overrun Daufuskie. The island is complicated to get to, pricey to stay on overnight, and very expensive to build upon. To top it off, we offer few opportunities to go shopping or otherwise dispose of casual money, yet everything costs more.

The rivers and the ocean isolate this place, make a fortress of it, in some respects. The Indians used Daufuskie for thousands of years. Their shell middens and village mounds line the riverbank at the heart of the island. The old plantation houses of the cotton barons are gone, but you can pick up hand forged nails and centuries old red and black clay bricks until you get bored. There is no bridge across the river and probably never will be. "The Water," as Pat Conroy said, "Is Wide." It takes a boat to get here. And that's one of the reasons I love it.

North, across Calibogue Sound, is Hilton Head. South, beyond Bloody Point, is Tybee Island. At night, the western shore of Daufuskie views the amber and yellow lights of Savannah. We islanders refer to the balance of North America as "The Other Side." And we do not especially like to go there.

Of course, folks who live in an isolated area usually regard strangers with suspicion. The first time I met Roger Pinckney, I thought he was an IRS investigator. He strolled into my backyard with a smile on his face, wearing for disguise a full beard, blue jeans and a pair of prescription sunglasses. The glasses were what seemed to give him away. They were large squares of almost black glass, appeared to be riding at a cocked angle on his nose. They were of outdated design and unfashionable shape, wire rimmed, the sort of quasi body armor issued to field operatives of shadow groups adherent to well known government agencies.

The odd angle at which the glasses rode the bridge of his nose suggested to me that whoever he was, the mission he was on superceded the details of personal appearance. He had the look of someone who would eat shark meat for breakfast for as long as it took to educate himself, and complete the mission. I couldn't remember having done anything wrong, but then I hadn't had a recognizable job since the Carter Administration, and here on Daufuskie it would be quite possible to miss out on news of an overthrow of human rights, to the extent that all Americans might now be required under the law to cash regular paychecks, and I had simply not been informed.

Roger's glasses were not on crooked; it just took me a while to realize, that he habitually and subtly cocks his whole head to a quizzical degree, as if the first question he will ask you is not quite formed, while the bent of your answer he seems to have already figured out.

His curiosity extends in strange directions. As soon as he told me his name, I connected him with the second book he wrote, called "Blue Roots," a factual history of the power and weirdness that arose when ancient African animism met European Christianity in the New World.

Here on Daufuskie, we are never far removed from Gullah mysticism, the religious heritage of "the root," otherwise and elsewhere referred to as Voodoo. When Roger Pinckney writes that spirits walk Daufuskie Island, that buzzards are transformed into eagles, or that he burned a "money candle," or tied his girlfriend's panties around some rare herb and hung the knot on his towel rack, he is not just whistling Dixie. Neither was his girlfriend, when she walked on fire and threw a cutting board at him rather than a knife.

He is the one white man I know of who is unafraid, or at least undaunted, when the headless chickens dance in Savannah and New Orleans.

The stories collected in *The Right Side of the River* are

recent history. They are a structure of clear, clean windows opening on a tiny world, geographically defined as a three by five mile barrier island. Daufuskie is the southernmost point in South Carolina, a state which happens to have been the most rebellious and seditious in the Federal Union, if memory serves. The political basis for the Civil War grew from planters indigenous to the low lying terrain and tidal estuaries so accurately, lovingly and ruthlessly rendered here. In *The Right Side of the River* you will meet the old boys, whose spiritual progenitors walked back down from Cemetery Ridge rather than let the Yankees see them run. You will also meet, in the literal flesh, descendants of slaves who are under attack by financial wizards, proud misguided profiteers, aground on the pluff mud, condemned by the root to economic dust. And the chained ancestors, now consigned to the spirit realm, whose consecrated hope and pagan ceremonies, doubtless, helped to defeat the armies of the Cotton Kingdom.

You will hear, or at least sense in the author's tone, the despair, the desperation, the endurance and vision of a fifty year old man committed to saving a tiny world from belated assault by the carpet baggers, the real estate agents of cultural doom, who arrive on the island wearing fashionable sunglasses, golf shirts and corporate veils, and who would transform Daufuskie Island into one more planned unit jungle.

Roger Pinckney was struck by lightning as a boy. Every day he lives is sacred to him. So is the act of writing, an exercise in romance, rage and wonder. His territory is here, on "The Right Side of the River." The facts don't get any stranger than this, nor the practice of journalism any more artful.

Dixie Crystals

The Capum sits on the edge of the bed, pale, skinny, and wild. He fixes me with the glare of an osprey.

"You hauling passengers or freight?" His voice is like a rusty bolt rattling around in a galvanized pail. Too many Camels, too much sour mash, too many years.

"Both, sir."

He considers that, then asks. "You hauling any sugar?"

"No sir."

"Promise me you won't haul any sugar."

The Capum is stuck in 1934. It's early spring and the Daufuskie moonshiners are low on corn and out of sugar and they are bringing Dixie Crystals over from Savannah in hundred pound sacks. The revenuers have gotten wind of it and the Capum worries I might get arrested.

So I promise.

But it's the winter of 2000 and the Capum is on the top rung. Dying of diabetes, angina, thrombosis, but mostly old age. I have sat with him an hour in his thousand dollar a day room, watched him choke on a scientifically perfect meal, but nevertheless not fit for a bluetick coonhound. Now I am getting ready to head home, to fight the traffic to Hilton Head on a highway more deadly than many small wars, to try to make the four o'clock ferry to Daufuskie.

The Capum is my daddy, riverman and engineer, who strung the spiderweb powerline to Daufuskie Island back in 1953. He built the county dock and power company dock and the oyster factory dock and the phone company dock. He was coroner and sheriff and so tough, one man swore to me, that he could set his plate on a dead man's face and eat his supper.

But he was even tougher than that. In thirty years, he pulled two dozen drowned boys out of the river and then he gave me a twelve foot bateau and set me loose upon it.

For him, it must have been like Abraham leading Isaac to the mountaintop. But this time there was no ram in the thicket. I got struck by lightning, fell overboard, swam with sharks and gators. I was lacerated, burned, swamped, marooned and cast ashore, a hundred times scared-to-Jesus death and shot at but never hit.

The river did not take my life, but the shimmering blue floodtide took my heart. The gurgling green suck in the low water creeks took my soul. If that were not enough, there was the glint of dawn upon the antlers of the rag-horned hummock bucks, the marsh hens cackling the tide change, the glory across the high marsh when the sun slips off toward Savannah.

The river took my heart and my soul but not my breath and I want to tell you all of it. The great tale of Indians and traders and slavers and the slaves and the voodoo drums. Of the pirates and the dope smugglers and the moonshiners and the Yankee army on the island we call Daufuskie. Of old Papy Burn who gave away his scuppernong wine after the revenuers told him he could no longer sell it. Of Miss Pauline, carrying on the tradition as best as she is able, selling beer off her back porch, slipping cans into box lunches of fried chicken and rice and okra.

I want to tell you, but I am only a man. I want to tell you about how the developers came and built a golf course and how Jack Nicklaus went to Miss Pauline's and did not know what okra was and Miss Pauline did not know who he was either. I want to tell you but sometimes I cry like an osprey and snort like a porpoise in a dead end creek and the words will just not come. But the moon is soon full and the surf is low and mumbling way off on the outer bars, distant thunder on the whispering wind and the spirit rises and speaks in the surf and the moon.

I cannot hear the surf here in this hospital room. There is the drone of the heat pump, muted conversation from the room next door and a nurse's squeaky shoes upon the hallway floor. But I know the moon is out there. I can feel it vibrate in sinew and bone. It tells me of things I know and things I wish I knew and I write in my heart as I sit with the Capum and wish he were fifty again and I sixteen. But I am fifty-four and he is ninety-one and dying and I am heading back to an island he taught me to love.

The moon must be working on the Capum, too, conjuring up his days on the river, even though he is not sure where he is right now. He struggles his legs back beneath the covers, lays deep into his pillow, looks out the window and speaks like he is reading the script off the sky. "Big celebration when the Savannah boats came in. *Clivedon, Merchant, Pilot Boy.* Whole island would turn out to see who got on and who got off, to help haul the sugar up into the woods. Sacks and sacks of Dixie Crystals, copper tubing, and Mason jars. They'd boil up shrimp and crabs and drink licker. Scrap iron licker. You know why they call it scrap iron?"

I do, but say I don't, not wanting to waste one last chance at a story I love. And the Capum, who will likely never get another drink of licker, wants to talk about it.

"Revenuers would be out in Field's Cut, hailing every bateau and smelling every lie. What you got on the boat, boy?" The Capum pauses, here on the last rung, still an artist, still spinning a world in air. "The licker was beneath all the engine blocks and radiators and fenders to sell the Jews over on Liberty Street. 'Scrap iron, suh, nothing but scrap iron.' That's what they called it so they would not lie."

The Capum is way off to starboard. I did that to my own kids, reading Bible stories till they knew them by rote and then having Moses stumble on a fish in his way across the Red Sea and kick it so hard it became a flounder with both eyes on the same side. And they would holler "No, Pa, Moses did not kick that fish!"

But my kids are grown and scattered all over and I am here with the Capum, a kid once again, and I cannot holler "No, Pa, no, tell me the rest of it," the way I know it in my heart.

So I wait for what comes next, how when the state men came aboard the deckhand winked at the mate, mate winked at the captain and there were six blasts instead of three when the boat came round the last bend. And then there was a great stampede up into the woods and the dust hung in the air from the oxcarts and Model A's and there wasn't even anybody left on the dock to pick up the mail.

But there are new stories in the Capum yet, and I do not know if he wants to tell them or if they have minds of their own and are breaking loose, slipping out before he and they are gone, except as I can remember and tell them later.

"You know your scrap iron, son?"

I got a nose for a story, and I got it from him. "No sir," I say.

"Look for those frog eyes."

"Yessir."

He looks out the window, south, over towards Parris Island; if the trees were not in the way he could see it, and see beyond to Port Royal Sound, blue, wide, and wonderful. And after that is Hilton Head, all jammed up now with houses and stores with little green strips everywhere to make you think you are deep in the woods. And beyond Hilton Head is Calibogue, treacherous as a two-hearted woman, and then there is Daufuskie, stuck in time.

"Roll the jar in your hand, watch it stick to the glass. Shake it and watch for bubbles. Big bubbles in pairs. Frog eyes."

"You can pour it into a bottle cap and burn it," I venture.

The Capum snorts, turns from the window and gives me another avian stare. "Gasoline will burn," is all he says.

And it will, but nothing like all this burning in my heart.

The Capum lays his hands across his chest, fingers sure but frail and gnarled and knotted. I can see my hands in them as surely as I see his face in mine. And one good story is all he can stand. He dozes, soon gently snores.

And I am left alone with the stories from the other side of the river. Stories from the grandchildren of those who ran, how some of them covered the stills and Grandma White, who knew hers was a goner, who just went for her bateau and struck out rowing for Savannah to buy what she needed to rebuild.

And Miss Pauline tending her mother's still with dried palmetto fronds, which burned quick and hot and made no smoke. And now fifty years later slipping beer into construction workers' bag lunches and still keeping an eye out for The State Man.

Two weeks before, I was down at the store, having a smoke and a cup of coffee with Skipper Billy while I waited on the mail. The mail comes on the ten o'clock boat in a couple of orange nylon bags. The pastor, with ten children but no church, picks it up and hauls it down to the post office. But the pastor was off the island that day and set a son to do it and he did not so we waited.

We waited and we talked about Ned The Pig and how the tourists buy a three dollar beer just to see him drink it, tusking open the can, holding it in his jaws, tipping his head back and steadily gulping whatever does not run down his jowls. But Ned was pushing three hundred with scant ground clearance and Skipper Billy was talking about switching him over to non-alcoholic brew when Joe Nathan came in the door.

Joe Nathan, Miss Pauline's boy, out of work and hungry and mostly thirsty. Thirty and thin and wild-eyed, beautiful and fierce, with a smile like a gator laying in the April sun. Once or twice a year Joe Nathan goes off on a Muslim tangent, zinging off into some inner cosmos, whirling like a dervish, quoting the Holy Koran and cussing the white race in invective worthy of Louis Farrakhan. And that day he was in the finest form. "God-damn the white man! I hate racism and I need a job so bad I'd choke somebody if they paid me to bury him."

But Skipper Billy knew how to handle it. He had seen Joe Nathan run screaming down the middle of Haig Point Road, speaking in tongues and calling it Arabic and hot-wiring a truck and scattering a covey of Yankee tourists on their Huffy single speeds. That morning, a little good humor went a long way and pretty soon we got the story. A contractor had piled the sad and tattered remains of two acres of woods close upwind to Miss Pauline's and had set it ablaze. His sister had wash on the line and threw it away. Miss Pauline could not breathe. Miss Cassie, right next door, lost three laying hens and a night's sleep from the howling dogs.

And I, who knew the Capum's stories, who loved this place, went home and called the Department of Health and Environmental Services and then went over to see Miss Pauline.

She hobbled around her kitchen, twissmout', as they say down here, shaking her head and mumbling to herself. The next morning, Joe Nathan was at my door. "Ain't nobody slept all night. Keep the State Man off my mama's porch."

I told Joe Nathan what I knew. The law said one thousand feet. If there was not a thousand feet between Miss Pauline's and the fire, they could not burn anymore. It did not matter whose porch the State Man walked on.

Joe Nathan went away greatly troubled. The state man came and he stood at the corner of the fire and shot the back corner of Miss Pauline's house with a range finder and it came up one hundred and seventy eight feet so he shut the burning down. He did not talk to Miss Pauline or Miss Cassie. Had he tried, they would have likely hobbled out the back door and stood in the palmetto thicket until he gave up and drove away.

The contractor sent a man to Miss Pauline's offering her money. Maybe she took it, maybe she did not. But it did not matter. The law was the law and for once the State Man came onto this island and he did not bust up stills. There are no more stills to bust up, just Miss Pauline, selling beer off her back porch.

After a few days when Miss Pauline had settled down and Miss Cassie was sleeping again, and the contractor was hauling away all the stumps he could not burn, I got an invitation to dinner, fried chicken or deviled crabs. I said some of both and ate them while Miss Pauline kept the sweet tea coming and the construction workers came to the back door and bought beer. And she asked about the Capum and said she would pray for him at the First African Baptist.

And I knew she would.

Now I watch him sleep, The Capum, my daddy, the man I love, the man who set me upon the waters, the man who gave me stories and the very breath to tell them.

I leave him there, still alive, and I drive to Bluffton and buy groceries, working my way down a mental list from eggs to grits to bacon. I get to the sugar and I stop and look at the crossbuck on the label, bold as the old Confederacy. Dixie Crystals. Old Fashioned Dark Brown, wonderful in chicory coffee. I need it and I want it but I do not buy it. I made a promise and I will stick to it.

And this is what happened the night the Capum was tee-tering on the top rung, ready to step off into Glory.

A Liberal Education

Y ou could fault the Capum many things. He cussed and he liked his licker and a pretty girl now and then and he never owned a boat that did not sink at least five times. But he knew his river and he loved me and fed me up good and he told me stories. And he helped me get some of my own, though it was considerable time before I came to appreciate the value of some of them, which is the way it is sometimes between fathers and sons.

The Capum painted signs during the Great Depression, told me how he lettered billboards saying See Rock City and Chew Brown's Mule and Drink Dixie Cola, hanging on a spiderweb of light lines because he could not carry a ladder on his bicycle. He put himself through Carolina in art and engineering, but then he took to the river, and never came out till he turned seventy-five and could no longer scamper up the rigging like turpentined coon.

But through it all the Capum believed in education. He said he had nearly hung himself getting one and—by God—he was going to hang me if I did not do the same. He got me to class on time and kept me there most days for four long years at Beaufort Senior High, a mile from the water but I could still smell it and it got me into trouble from time to time when I cut class to crab or throw a net. And then the Capum sent me off to Carolina, where, to his great dismay, I came home with some ideas he did not entirely appreciate.

But that all came later. Right then I was in high school and the Capum was of the mudbank solid persuasion that public education had no monopoly on the educational process. He was right, of course, and entirely correct in springing me to hunt deer and maybe quail and, for sure, marsh hens on the September new moon tide. But then there were times when he needed an extra deckhand on the barge, which he did frequently, and often to my great discomfort.

Mama would generally bring the news. I would be innocently brushing my teeth and slicking up for school and thinking about my ever pressing adolescent responsibilities and she would stick her head in the bathroom door and ask, "How would you like to help your father today?"

Mama, like the Capum, had a wheelbarrow of her own faults, but she played me like any woman plays a man, keeping me from the Capum's cussing squalls one minute, then being a one-woman press gang the next.

So it was not really a question. Or maybe it was. Technically, it was not if I were going, but if I would like it. I generally did not, but that did not matter. I'd chew my toothbrush and wait for the Capum to stroll into the bedroom and cut an eye in my direction and peek out the window at the wet Spanish moss moving in the sea wind and pronounce, "'S'pose to dee-minish."

He always said that and he was right about half the time. There were complications that morning—a spelling test, heavy laden with four syllable words, for which I was ill prepared. I was also considering the Capum's orders—take *Sweet*

Bedelia down to Daufuskie and haul a barge and a broken down school bus back to Bluffton.

There was the spelling test and then there was Calibogue. Blue, wide, and wonderful, it could turn mean in an instant, especially when a stiff east wind got to kicking up swells on an ebb tide. I've heard old time tug skippers call it the roughest crossing on the East Coast and from what I've seen, I believe them.

So I came to a compromise. Sort of. I would go, only because I must. And I would carry the spelling book, as duty said I should. I would study underway, and make up the test tomorrow. But the words I was responsible for that day, I never learned, so even now I cannot relate them to you without appearing illiterate.

Five minutes later, we were loaded up and rolling, rolling in a rattly old one ton Chevy, bilge pumps, life jackets, hanks of rope and monkey wrenches and big hammers and pinch bars and oars and what-all crammed onto the back bed.

The Capum took Carteret down to the corner of Bay and picked up Cuffey Dawes who had hitchhiked to the foot of the Lady's Island bridge from one of the islands. Cuffey had worked for the Capum since before I was born, and my grandfather before that. He was an all round Gullah riverman, one of the best. He could look at the moon and tell you when the shrimp would run, flip over a leaky bateau, drive oakum into the seams, scull out into a dead end creek and come back with a bucket of prawns before breakfast. He played a mean game of bottlecap checkers and kept a pipe to run the lowtide gnats and the only things that spooked him were rattlesnakes and ghosts and you could depend on him in a tight spot, so long as no reptiles or spirits were involved.

Sweet Bedelia was a WWII seaplane tender and getting a little weak along the seams. In her better days, with half a tank of fuel and the 671 Jimmy wound up tight, it would plane off and win cases of beer in races from Bay Street to Bay Point. But by the time I was old enough to work her, she took on water overnight and wheezed and coughed and you could see her twist and flex in heavy seas and she wouldn't quite plane off anymore, just waller and roar and throw one hell of a wake. She was tied at the county dock at Bluffton, thirty feet, flatbottomed, stove sided and leaky. The Capum broke out the bilge pumps and Cuffey and I labored over them while he poured fuel from five gallons cans and fired her up and she blubbered and smoked while we pumped. Then I got the bateau off the bank and tied it tight amidships with a light manila line. We cast off and headed down the May River for Daufuskie.

It was near flood tide and the Capum chose Cauley's Creek over Calibogue. If you look at Cauley's on a chart, it looks like an easy run, but charts don't always tell the whole story. It winds between Palmetto Bluff Plantation and Bull Island, down to the Cooper River and Ram's Horn Creek, another tricky piece of water, especially if you meet a pulpwood barge halfway through. Cauley's has sand bars where they shouldn't be, and shell rakes like piles of razor blades that can take the prop right off a motor and cypress snags that have been knocking bottoms out of boats for a hundred years.

But the Capum knew his water and we made it through Cauley's and Ramshorn and headed on down the New River. Cuffey beat me twice at bottlecaps, let me beat him once. The rain slacked off but the wind was up, so I kept the spelling book beneath my slicker, out of the spray coming over the bow.

We made Daufuskie about lunchtime and Lance Burn met us at the end of his dock with a sack of baloney sandwiches and Dixie Colas, which were almost like a Coke, but twice as big and only cost a nickel. Lance Burn was king of Daufuskie. He owned thirty acres on the river. He was magistrate. He was white. He had a sheriff's department radio, the only communication back when there were no phones. He had a shrimp boat rigged to haul freight over from Savannah, and an ancient Ford flatbed, which was exactly half the trucks on the island. He was married to Miss Billie, the postmaster who also drove the school bus when it was running. When it wasn't, Lance hauled the kids on his flatbed.

The bus wasn't running that day, or that month, so far as I know. It was aboard a sad and buckled barge, tied down with bits of cast off line and chocked with a couple of pieces of split oak stovewood. The swaybacked old derelict was pulled up into the New River marsh and tied to a couple of oaks so it wouldn't sink overnight. But the tide was high and Cuffey got one oar onto the bateau transom and sculled up through the marsh and got a line on her and we snorted and bored until we got her off into deep water. Then the Capum put Cuffey aboard with one of the hand pumps to keep her afloat on the way home.

So we ate the baloney sandwiches and drank the Dixie Colas and waved goodbye to Lance and Miss Billie and our little flotilla headed up the New River—*Sweet Bedelia* with bateau lashed close astern, then the old barge with the school bus trailing behind on fifty feet of hawser, Cuffey puffing his pipe and methodically working the bilge pump.

The tide was dropping fast and we fought the current all the way to Ramshorn. The creek got its name from being so terribly crooked and narrow. Back before I was born, the Corps of Engineers dredged it straighter, but not much wider. And we met a pulpwood tow half way through.

She was *Roletta* out of Charleston, pulling umpteen thousand pounds of slash pine down to the mill at Savannah, all yellow and bleeding turpentine down the steel on the water washed side of the hull. She drew a lot of water and carried a lot more with her—a great bulge in the surface of the cut— and I could see the water rush out of the little side creeks as she passed.

The Capum had been aboard her once, and said she was powered by twin locomotive diesels. And being next to her in the narrow cut was like being in a tunnel with a thundering freight. She had five feet of white water in front of the first barge and she blew for a port passing and we gave her all the room we could. The Capum kept us hard against the east bank and I could feel the prop vibrate when it found mud when *Roletta* drew the river down.

By the time we made it out of Ramshorn, the tide was too low for Cauley's. We'd have to run Calibogue and I saw soon enough it would be a rough crossing. We ran into heavy chop as we cleared the last point before big water. I had the bateau close astern, tied with a hank of line about as good as the rest of the Capum's equipment. The bateau was a heavy old hog, five quarter cypress and waterlogged to the heart. Each time *Bedelia* rose on a swell, the bateau would fall into the trough behind and give the line a good snap. It wasn't long before it parted.

I had my nose in the spelling book and I did not see it go. I looked up when I heard Cuffey holler and saw him make a snatch at it as it blew by. The Capum started cussing and throttled down and waved me forward to take the wheel. I came a bit to port, held her into the wind while the Capum went astern and bellered back and forth with Cuffey.

The Capum came back to the wheel again and eased *Bedelia* toward Haig Point. There's a lighthouse there, all fixed up now for the tourists to come marvel at. But in those days half the shakes were gone, the clapboards peeling, and the windows busted out. But the old dock to land groceries for the keeper and kerosene for the light was still standing. And the Capum had a plan, as usual. He would swing by on the ebbtide, just close enough for Cuffey to make the jump. Cuffey would follow the bateau until it blew ashore. The Capum would hold us out in Calibogue till Cuffey rowed out to meet us.

It was a good plan, excepting details. We were low on fuel and Cuffey could not swim. Then there was the seepy barge, desperately needing Cuffey's attention. But the Capum knew his business and Cuffey jumped and he made it and we blubbered away out in Calibogue while he chased the bateau on foot. I put down the spelling book and got the binoculars and watched it go, pitching and rolling on the swells, the oars still in the oarlocks and the handles sticking above the gunnel like goat horns. Then I caught Cuffey in the fine green haze of the riverbank, running with a driftwood stick, stopping to beat hell out of every briar tangle before plunging through it. Then he rounded a point of wax myrtle and was gone.

The Capum hollered and pointed to the barge. She was

riding low, staggering with each new swell, the bus working at its lashings, rolling two inches, now three, against the stove-wood chocks. The Capum pulled an ax from the locker and sent me aft again to the stern cleat. He hollered against the wind and the engine rattle. "Watch them hatches, son. If they blow, cut her loose 'fore she pulls us down, too."

So I sat, wet and then wetter, me and the spelling book and the ax and the hawser and a creation of cold gray water and a line that would cut me clean in two if it broke on the other end before I could cut it on mine. But the bus stayed put and the line did not part and the barge kept floating, if just barely. An hour later, I saw Cuffey clear the top of a big swell, a mile or more away, leaning into the oars, spray breaking clean over the top of the bateau. He was as wet as I was but his pipe was still lit and he blew a great puff of blue smoke into the wind when he leaned into each stroke, like a steam locomotive on a long uphill pull. Then he disappeared into the trough and all I could see was smoke until he labored up the next wave.

I jumped aboard when he came alongside, slipping and sliding and falling into the slimly bilge of the bateau, now six inches deep with seawater. There might have been some small part of me that was still dry, in a place I'd hesitate to mention. If there was, that fall took care of it. But I had little chance to consider that indignity. I jumped back up, got busy with the oars, put Cuffey back on the barge, then came back alongside *Bedelia* and tied her up again, giving her more slack this time.

The Capum hollered for me to take the wheel again while he crawled forward to check the tanks, dipping into them with a piece of lath marked with a carpenter's pencil. He came back to the wheel shaking his head. "We're low on fuel. Tide will be with us in the May River. That'll help."

We pushed on across Calibogue, rounded that big marshy point off Barataria Island, then headed up the May River. The tide had changed and we were out of the worst of the swells. Cuffey was back on the pump and the barge was sitting higher and not wallering around so bad. The tide was about two hours into the flood, something to see in the narrows of the May, where twice each day ten feet of water rushes to flood thirty thousand acres of marsh and the current runs like a millrace. We fairly flew along.

I fetched out the spelling book and took a stab at a few words, but it was hard to keep at it, the great misty jumble of points and islands slipping by like that, the great panorama of my youth, the shoreline deep and green and wonderful, a single house every so often, stately and white and framed by the moss hung oaks, those things that were vanishing though I did not know it yet. And the river murmured and Cuffey thumped away at the pump and blew clouds of blue smoke and the diesel purred along and then quit. It did not grumble, backfire, belch or pop. It did just like diesels do when they run out of fuel. Quit, bam, right now, without warning, just like you had shut them off with a switch.

The Capum danced on one foot, then the other. He started cussing, pulled off his cap and waved it around, but he did not throw it down and jump up and down on it the way my uncle did when they dug his basement too big. By and by the cussing died down and the Capum put his hat back on and took up coherent communication again. "Skipper, get below and break out the outboard. Get it on the bateau and get

Cuffey off the barge."

I jumped to it. The motor was an old eighteen Evinrude and heavy as hell. I wrestled it up and over the side and got it clamped onto the bateau without rupturing myself, a minor miracle. It took a dozen pulls to get it going, some fiddling and—since I was too young to cuss around the Capum—some very private profanity as well. Bluffton was coming up fast by the time I got Cuffey back aboard. We had both the wind and the tide behind us now and the old bus was acting like a sail. Getting to Bluffton was no longer a problem, but how to stop once we arrived most certainly was.

The Capum scrambled down into the bateau, began nudging us—bateau, *Bedelia,* bus, and barge—toward the county dock, a mile or so upriver. Just beyond the dock was a private wharf with a million dollar sloop and then there were shrimp boats at anchor and a two mile stretch of riverbank with a rickety dock every hundred yards or so.

"All I can do is steer her," the Capum yelled. "I'll get her close and you get a line on that dock!" He paused and cussed again. "You'll only get one chance!"

Cuffey and I went forward and got the stoutest line we could get a hold of in a hurry. Cuffey, God bless him, whipped a bowline loop into the end before you could say it, and swung the rope like he was about to rodeo a calf. I was glad it was him and not me. Missing meant hitting the sloop, and then a shrimp boat, or two, then a collection of match stick docks until we found something that would hold us or we went down.

We were doing five knots when we swung by the county dock, about twenty feet out, the little eighteen churning and bucking and doing the best it could. Cuffey slung underhand and the loop blossomed out like a cowboy's lasso and snagged a piling on the downtide corner. I made the other end fast and got away with all my fingers while *Bedelia* ate up the slack.

Forty-odd years later, I can close my eyes and still see that line take the load, pulling down down as it stretched, the water instantly wrung from its fiber and hanging in the air around it in a fine gray mist. There was no time to jump and for one terrifying second I thought it would part and blow me and Cuffey to Kingdom Come—the Gullah riverman and the Capum's boy, together forever, though both in pieces. But then I felt the boat slip sideways beneath me and *Sweet Bedelia* and the barge and the bateau neatly swung around, missing the stern of the sloop by a dozen feet.

It was business as usual for the Capum, long on work, short on equipment. He did not leap and holler and praise Jesus like Cuffey did. He did not get down and kiss the timbers on the county dock like I wanted to do and would have done had he not been there.

I squished ashore, leaving soggy tracks on a deck that seemed to heave and wobble like Calibogue Sound. The Capum went for a can of fuel. I was planning to get back to my spelling but Cuffey sat me down under an oak and talked me into a game of bottlecap checkers, which he won. The Capum came back and I hauled the fuel aboard and he went below to bleed the filters. Then we fired her up and put the barge on the bank and made her fast to a couple of oaks. We tied up the *Sweet Bedelia,* pumped her down one last time and headed back to Beaufort in the truck.

Halfway home, I remembered the spelling book. It was

right where I left it, safe and dry in the locker with the charts. I didn't say anything and Cuffey puffed on his pipe and the Capum kept driving.

Heart Pine

There are special times and special places and sometimes they come together in special ways, like God Himself was doing the arranging, pulling light and weaving air and moving earth and sky and sea just to make you weep from wonder.

Like when the tide rises to brimming full and the moon comes up over Grenadier Shoals and the wind drops off to a whisper and the sea flattens and you can hear the gong-gong of the bell buoys way out in the mouth of Port Royal Sound. Or when you're hard aground in a little side creek and you wait and wait on the new tide to turn you loose and all at once the barnacles pop and the marsh hens cackle and you see the water swap directions and your soul sings and your blood swaps directions, too.

All this and more, a thousand times ten thousand blessings. The great rafts of sea ducks bobbing white and black out beyond the surf line, the plovers and sanderlings racing down the surging backwash, skittering up the beach with each new wave, the mullet flashing silver along the sand bar and the osprey that falls among them like feathered lightning.

I was born to all this glory, the eleventh Roger Pinckney in a line that has called this place home for two hundred and fifty years. Roger IV, grandfather with more greats than I have room to write, came here from Peterborough England, Deputy

Provost Marshal of Carolina, a Servant of the King. Weary of enforcing increasingly unenforceable decrees, he switched sides and joined the rabble in throwing off the English yoke. He married Susannah Hayne, of the lineage that later debated Daniel Webster. His cousin Charles signed the Constitution, as did his other cousin Charles Cotesworth, Secretary of War and later State. His great-grandson Roger VII fired upon Fort Sumter and started what we call down here The War Between the States.

A scant five-two with a size three shoe, my great-grandfather volunteered to serve aboard the *Hunley,* the hand-cranked Confederate submarine that took every crew down with her but sank a Yankee ship on her last run. He was not chosen, and when they finally got the *Hunley* up one hundred and thirty-odd years later, great-grandpa's bones were not among those they found, thank God.

I tell you this for reference only and I want no credit for it. When I was younger and my father wanted to groom me for the United States Senate, I considered this lineage more of a curse than anything, and I sometimes schemed of adopting a black baby and naming him Roger Pinckney XII.

But I made my own Roger Pinckney XII, in a steaming shower in a rickety farmhouse in far away Minnesota, when the wind rattled the shingles and the snow piled to the windowsills and the water off our bodies froze when it slopped out onto the bathroom floor.

But before that I made Susannah Hayne Pinckney, and Shelley Hanna Pinckney, and Laura Elaine Lyseng Pinckney, the littlest girl with the longest name. I would scoop her from her bed at 2:00 A.M. and bundle her against the deadly cold, and take her into the snowy yard and show her the northern lights popping and crackling and rolling like Pentecostal fire. I read her all the Little House books before she was able to read them herself and she grew up like the rest of them did—on horseback by the time she was three, killing deer at twelve, and breaking hearts by fifteen, a Southerner who talked like a Yankee, eating venison and grits and tomatoes and gumbo made of freshwater panfish rather than saltwater shrimp.

Roger XII's momma wanted a home birth and I did not. She went into labor in the pickup and I was heading for the hospital and she made me take her home to get her toothbrush first. When it took her three contractions to negotiate the front steps, I knew I had been had. So I laid her on the little cot in the extra bedroom and turned on the lights, but a beaver had dropped a tree on the lines and the lights did not work. Neither did the pump. But there was a kettle of hot water upon the stove from the last batch of canned tomatoes, so I washed my hands and got ready for another little Pinckney—another *Pinkette,* my friends used to say.

The phone still worked and before I got down to my chores, I called around trying to find the preacher so he could come watch the rest of the kids while I delivered the last of them. I called the church and the general store and finally the bar and pretty soon the yard was full of pickups full of men full of beer awaiting the results.

The labor was hard but quick and when my namesake slid out between his mother's lovely quivering thighs, he looked blue and lifeless in the dead-and-dug-up-again light of the hissing Coleman lantern. But one breath and he was wriggling and screaming and pink and I tied off his cord with fishing line and cut it with my skinning knife and wrapped him in a towel and walked out onto the porch and held him aloft and hollered "It's a boy!"

And the men in the pickups whooped and cheered and hollered "Pinckney, have a beer!"

And I had three.

But I was telling you about Grenadier Shoals and the rolling blue beauty of Port Royal Sound, where the tide plays tunes on your anchor line and devilfish as big as your garage door and as heavy as your car leap clear of the water and smack down again like the crack of lightning. And of the bell buoys that tolled for me.

There's a little line of beach shacks along the north shore, at a place called Land's End. If you are ever blessed to see that water, look hard through the sea haze and count from the east, one, two, three, four, you'll find the one where I spent my summers as a kid.

My daddy, Capum Roger X, built it of Carolina heart pine in 1950 when I was four years old. He tore down one of the old barracks on Parris Island and barged the lumber across to Land's End and built it there upon the river beach, a thousand square feet with a broad screen porch and paneling scarred from fifty years of Marine recruits amusing themselves by throwing bayonets at the wall. There was a fireplace of brick from the salvaged barracks chimney where we started fires with pinecones, fed them heart pine from the scrap pile at the edge of the yard and, finally, branches from the oaks across the road, stripped from living trees by the last hurricane.

Heart pine was hard to come by in 1950, today impossible. Laid up where you can see it, in floors and paneling and exposed rafters, it looks more stone than wood. Down where the copperheads and black snakes coil, in the dusty dark beneath the house, carpenter ants can't eat it and termites try, but soon give up in disgust, jaws gummed, intestines plugged with yellow sap hard as amber.

You'll never see heart pine, unless you tear down a building like my daddy did. Marketable stands of heart pine, longleaf pine, like the giant bald cypress, have gone the way of the Carolina Parakeet and the Ivory Billed Woodpecker, the Florida Panther, and the Louisiana Black Bear, fatalities all to the Progress of Man.

But I was talking about the shack on the Land's End beach, not the long leaf stand cut down before my daddy was born. Summer times, we'd use the little shack the most. About a week before school let out, Daddy would pull his deckhands off the barge and choose a lowtide afternoon and set them grubbing out the stobs and snags the winter storms had exposed out on the beach. When the tide rose they'd tackle the tangle that would become a yard once again and the Daddy would tinker with the pump until it sucked water too brackish for anything but showers and dishes and then the place would be ready once again. And a week later Momma would pack the station wagon with groceries and towels and kids and Land's End would be home for a couple of months.

Given a choice, Momma liked an ocean beach, Hunting or Edisto islands. Nearly everything else dissatisfied her. And I mean everything. She lost her daddy when she was four and came up poor in the Great Depression, the daughter of a hardworking female journalist. Maybe that got her off on the wrong foot. She grumbled her way through life, and the few times I remember her happy is when she walked on the beach and looked out at the waves.

But the ocean beach is a cruel place. It's hot in the summer and cold in the winter and the blow-sand gets into your sandwiches and between your teeth and places I would not want to mention and there is no shade or shelter anywhere. Give me a river beach like Land's End, where the little waves lap and whisper and the tide murmurs secrets only those who love it can hear.

We swam and crabbed and fished and collected shells and roamed the woods and pulled Indian pottery out of the bank where Swash Creek cuts deep into the mud as it snakes up toward Tombee Plantation. Once I had a hat full of shards and a friend of my mother's had none, so she sat in the sand and pouted and said she would sit right there and dig until she found an arrowhead. We kids walked away giggling and she sat and dug with her hands no more than two feet and came up with a beautiful little point, flint the color of a Cherokee rose.

Way beyond Land's End is Bay Point Island, a tattered and windblown two hundred acre scrap of creation God must have had second thoughts about, since He set the sea thundering against it and He knew the sea always won.

The ocean rolled Bay Point back upon the marsh, year by year, relentlessly, as surely as you roll a rug. The beach moved, the dunes moved, the scrub brush fell into the sea but quickly sprouted and grew again on the new dunes. But the hundred foot pines did not, and they toppled and lay in the surging surf, ghostly postscripts to an island's passing.

On full moon low tides when the water went way, way

down and a west wind took it down further, you could walk out a mile or more onto a sandspit on the island's north end and if you were lucky you could find the old brass wellheads, polished bright by the scouring sand, and you knew there were once houses there and you realized how far the island had washed in a hundred years.

Bay Point was where I went after the well finally went sour. Daddy sold the beach shack for five thousand dollars. I begged him not to do it. I cried piteously, even though I was ten years old. My uncle ran a well rig. Couldn't he just drill us a new one?

Daddy explained. Beaufort County was growing. They were taking out more water than the ground could stand. Sweetwater, coming all the way down from the distant Blue Ridge, could not keep up and, far offshore, saltwater was moving through cracks in the sea floor to make up the difference. Wells all over the islands were going bad, those closest to the sea first.

In another dozen years, they would dig a canal from the Savannah River and build a treatment plant by the Chechessee bridge, bringing water with traces of iridium and plutonium from the leaky Barnwell nuclear plant to Beaufort and Port Royal and Parris Island, and then the wells would slowly sweeten once again. The beach shack Daddy sold for five thousand dollars would eventually be for sale again for over a quarter million.

But he did not know that then and I did not know that then and I cried and wrung my hands and Daddy went off in private and changed his will to make me beneficiary of a term life insurance policy that would never be worth a damn since he lived well into his nineties. But neither of us knew that then, either.

Momma might have cried, too, though I never saw it. Next summer, Daddy rented us a house on Hunting Island, but only for ten days. Next year, it was a week. But the next year I turned thirteen and I got my first outboard motor and I was turned loose upon the river and eventually, the world.

Before the motor there were oars and a cypress bateau that Daddy must have chosen for its high transom and deep skeg and no place where a motor might fit. Playing tide and wind, I rowed all over my little bit of creation, exploring Brickyard Point, eating bag lunches over on Goat Island, skinny-dipping on the sandbar in front of Miss Lilly's house.

Miss Lilly Lindberg was my first introduction to the Swedish race, twenty years before I went bumming up in Minnesota and got tangled up with a long string of Scandinavian girls. She was my kindergarten teacher, and later my guardian when I went skinny-dipping on her sandbar. She thought it was her sandbar, anyway, and she thought it was her river, too. She would jealously guard both with a long-barreled Colt pistol, standing on the bank, gaunt and severe, in her ankle length schoolmarm dress, hair up in a kerchief, screaming warnings and then letting fly at passing boats. Once in a while her bullets thunked into a crabber's or a water skier's hull and Miss Lilly would receive a visit from the sheriff, also a former student.

But I was talking about my first boat. Eventually, that bateau was replaced with a sixteen foot Yellow Jacket molded plywood skiff and a wheezy eighteen Evinrude Fastwin with a distinctly unpleasant noise in the lower unit.

We called it Bumblebee. And it stung too, when you ran it in the rain and the magneto leaked juice out into the tiller. I'd take off my shirt and insulate my hand, but soon enough the rain and spray would make a connection again and you'd get a feeling like you get in church when the spirit starts working and I'd turn the shirt over and try to find a dry spot and that would work a little while longer.

But in good weather, you could take it far offshore and troll for mackerel and blues till the tall pines along the beach lay on the horizon like a fine green smudge. You could auger though pluff mud and sand and jump a shell rake or two and ball the propeller up with ropy marshgrass and if you had a handful of shear pins and a pair of channel locks and maybe a spare sparkplug and an emery board for the points, Bumblebee would always get you home.

I was a high school freshman when I took Bumblebee and the Yellow Jacket up a sinuous creek behind Bay Point. There was Jim and Eddie and Beekman, refugees from the No Trespassing signs that were springing up on islands and hummocks all over Beaufort County, and me still looking to fill that hole in my heart where a Land's End beach shack used to be.

There was a line of low hummocks out there in the high marsh, a string of old dunes from when the sea level dropped at the end of the last Ice Age. It was poor ground, supporting only cedar, palmettoes, a few scraggly pines, beach grass, cassina, and wax myrtle snake brush. The creek wound non-committally off to the southwest, then swung east, then south again. I idled down and let the tide pull us along, Bumblebee shaking and blubbering and sending smoky exhaust bubbles into the turgid green water.

Eddie and Jim and Beekman stood on their seats and peered above the spartina and I knew what they were thinking. There were perhaps a thousand little hummocks in the county, but very few accessible by deep water. We waited and wondered where this creek might take us.

It took us right where we needed to be, a steep cutbank right next to the tail end of the last hummock. Perfect.

"Hang on, boys," I said.

They did and I hit the throttle and Bumblebee roared and the skiff shot up onto the mud.

We clambered ashore, with no less relief than Columbus' crew must have felt when they finally got onto that beach in the Bahamas. But there were no bare-titted native girls to meet us, just clouds of sand gnats, which set upon us in a frenzy. We poked around in the brush, swatting and scratching, weather eyes out for moccasins and copperheads. We knew there would be no water here, nor any firewood, but there was a little hillock of high ground between a palmetto, a pine, and a bullet shaped red cedar—a good spot for a shack, if the bugs didn't eat you alive.

Finally, the gnats drove us back to the boat. Out on deep blue water, spinning back upriver, we laid our plans. We'd build a little dock out to deep water, nothing fancy, just fenceposts, 2 x 6 stringers and pallets for decking. Jim knew where he could get roofing tin, Beekman, some windows and doors. Eddie could get ahold of some salvaged siding. The joists and sills and rafters were my department.

I already had that covered. Back behind Daddy's shop on Pigeon Point road was a pile of lumber beneath a rotting tarp. It had been there a dozen years, still sound, timbers from the

Parris Island barracks, left over from the shack at Land's End.

Heart pine.

We hauled all of it down to the hummock, trip after trip, sixteen miles down the Beaufort River and Port Royal Sound in our little skiffs. We laid it upon the ground, squared it up as best we could. We spiked it together with a hammer we called The Big Bopper and case-hardened nails brittle as watch springs. The wood was hard and the nails were hard and the hammer was heavy and the nails would sometimes break— shatter, actually. *Vipp,* they took off through the air like .22 bullets; *tick,* landing way out in the marsh. It's a God's wonder nobody lost an eye.

It took us two years. When we were done, we had a bunkhouse with a broad screen porch, an old time icebox, gutters feeding an overhead shower tank, a Dixie No Smoke range, and a generator that worked most of the time. We called it the Gale Break Camp from the wild surf plunging and rolling a few hundred yards across the high marsh. I fancied it looked a bit like the Land's End beach shack.

Too soon 1962 became 1965 and since there was a war over in Vietnam all of us went off to college, to defer, at least for a while, that dreaded letter that began "Greeting."

The camp finally completed, I did not want to go far. I enrolled at USCB, the local branch of the University of South Carolina, and spent every free weekend at Gale Break. Christmas, 1965 was the best. We ate oysters, got into the spottails in the surf, took a raghorned buck up on Bay Point. Christmas morning, when I ventured to the outhouse at dawn, I found the cedar behind the house loaded with migrating monarch butterflies. When the sun slipped up over the dunes and the butterflies felt the first scant heat, they slowly opened and closed their wings and the cedar pulsed like a thing aflame, green to yellow, green to orange, God once again smiling and pulling the strings.

Merry Christmas, boys.

But then there was Faysal bin Abd al-Aziz bin Abd al-Rahman Al Saud. It would be years before I found out his full name. Back then we called him "that A-rab fornicator," but we did not use fornicator.

Prince Faysal would one day inherit the throne of Saudi Arabia. Meanwhile, he was cruising the world in his seagoing yacht and he needed an East Coast anchorage. Bay Point Island was perfect and he bought it for five million dollars.

We got a letter from a slick Charleston lawyer with a Broad Street address, a place Daddy called Shark Alley, offering us a five-year lease on our campsite for one dollar.

We knew the law, or the lack of the law, in such instances. Nobody knew if our hummock was part of Bay Point Island. If we signed the lease, we would acknowledge that it was and could have five more years of this blue and gold and green glory. If we did not, and could hang on for another two years, we could file a deed, pay taxes and Gale Break would be ours forever.

We did not sign.

Six months before the magic seven years, someone torched the Gale Break Camp. I was not there to see it burn, but I heard you could see the leaping flames for miles.

Heart pine makes one hell of a fire.

Daufuskie Dirt

"If you want to hear 'bout ghos'," Miss Pauline says, "Go talk to Tyrone. He see 'em mos' ever day."

We are sitting on Miss Pauline's porch, mouths full of her famous fried chicken, while temporarily more fortunate chickens squawk and peck and scratch in the dirt of Miss Pauline's clean swept yard. There's me and Miss Judi and Dave from The Learning Channel, down on Daufuskie Island scouting locations for a Halloween special.

I live here and Miss Judi is trying to live here and Dave gave me a check from his boss to use my connections to get him where most white folks cannot go.

And so we're down on Daufuskie, halfway between Hilton Head and Savannah. Timbered, green and beautiful, now and forever bridgeless, stuck in time. Call it 1956, call it 1936, give up and just shrug and call it Daufuskie, a place like nowhere else on earth.

Papy Burn, the keeper of the Bloody Point Light from 1898 until 1925, and island resident for the rest of his long and colorful life, waxed poetic when he met the governor in 1955. "I wouldn't trade a teaspoon of Daufuskie dirt for the whole state of South Carolina."

Daufuskie. Pat Conroy wrote about it, Jimmy Buffett sang about it, and the developers who have gobbled up Hilton

Head and Fripp and a dozen other islands want it.

They want it, but they can't quite make it pay. In 1980, they bit off a sizeable chunk, but acres got stuck in their throats when costs of an hour ferry ride pushed projects far into the red. A couple of hundred million later, one developer sold out for a buck, others struggled with foreclosure.

So we eat chicken and fried okra and butter beans this lovely spring day. And we are stuck in time while the irises bloom in the cool green woods and the bull 'gators burp about their social prospects and the warblers twitter about their fine wintertime in the Antilles.

We eat fried chicken while interest accrues and executives do battle with numbers and hypertension and ulcers and the surf mumbles off in the distance, way off at Melrose, Bloody, and Haig Point plantations, where you can't go unless you belong. While the myrtle and bay and magnolia green up along the back-island creekside, giving lush refuge for an eclectic community of shrimpers, artists, dope smokers, and self-proclaimed river rats.

But it's the middle of the island that has brought us to Miss Pauline's porch—land tenuously held by the Gullah, the descendants of Daufuskie's plantation-era slaves. This is where the night air seethes with silent rhythms of the Other Side, of West Africa. Where window frames and doorposts sometimes bear a brilliant haint blue to keep plentiful spirits at bay. Where cattle are kept, not for milk or meat, but as a sign of status. Where graves in the old cemeteries all face east, so the dead may "fly 'way home" if they want. Where the great liquid Gullah tongue confounds the untutored with all it's syncopations, contractions, and poetry.

Miss Pauline, umpteenth generation islander, saw this lurching transition from Afro-backwater to nearly successful golf retreat from the kitchen of the Melrose Plantation real estate office, where in five years she fried 10,000 pounds of chicken and unnumbered bushels of okra that sold $25,000,000 worth of real estate. Bobby Burn—Papy's grandson and wry and astute observer of this great cultural clash—pegged it perfectly. "There's something about Miss Pauline's fried chicken that makes a man want to spend money."

Maybe there was more to Miss Pauline's chicken than seven secret spices. There is a story about Miss Pauline and Capum Bob. Capum Bob threw a stowaway off the Melrose ferry, then got a voodoo doll in the mail, strategically run through with long hatpins. Capum Bob threw it in the trash and, subsequently, lost the engine in his four-wheel-drive Ford, then his job. When his wife went to Miss Pauline for a little consultation, his run of bad luck ceased.

This is what we are after in a bit of reverse psychology. We would spend some money and praise her twenty-five million dollar chicken and Miss Pauline would reciprocate.

Talking about such things requires considerable finesse. Talk about those things and they might get you. The hag—the female who slips her skin and becomes invisible and straddles you in your sleep and smothers you with her private parts. The plateye—the trickster who assumes forms you do not suspect until it is far too late. The jack-mulater—the ghost light that sneaks up out of the swamp and scares the bejesus out of you when you are walking down the Daufuskie dirt road minding your own business and thinking about sweet brown girls and moonshine liquor.

"Miss Pauline, do you know any old stories about the island?"

"What kinda stories?"

Go easy, now, real easy. "You know, ghost stories...."

Then came the non-committal Gullah grunt and her mouth snapped shut like a bull 'gator.

But then there was the suggestion to go find Tyrone.

Like Julius Caesar, Tyrone was "born with de caul," the amniotic sack over his eyes. The Romans took this as a sign of impending greatness, but the Gullah know it gives you "de sight."

And Tyrone is indeed a man who sees things a bit differently. When the Haig Point Lifter was going to charge him $150 to bring his boat trailer onto the island, Tyrone ran the boat onto the trailer, cut it loose from the truck, and ran the skiff over 20 miles of deep blue water with the trailer strapped beneath. "Sure I had to replace the bearing, but that be cheaper than ferry." When his "bully"—his calf that he was going to train to pull a cart—was not faring well on the typical Daufuskie diet of dirt and nothing, Tyrone loaded it onto the skiff and took it 40 miles to St. Helena Island, where a cousin had a lush, green pasture. The bully did well and eight months later, when his cousin called him to come and get it, it weighed well over a thousand pounds.

The tribulation of the return trip was predictable. After nearly kicking the bottom out of the boat, the bully broke loose a mile from shore, jumped overboard, swam through the waving saltmarsh and escaped into the woods. After the round-up, Tyrone wrapped the bully's head in his rainjacket, whispered soothing words in Gullah and continued the journey. The bully, now a full grown ox, but still unbroken to harness, eats Daufuskie dirt and drinks nothing while tethered in Tyrone's front yard, kept company by seven shaggy goats, and a flock of scrabbling chickens.

But like just about everything and everybody and every place on this island so securely stuck in time, there is something else about Tyrone. When provoked by the moon and moonshine—"scrap iron," they call it down here—Tyrone has a habit of taking off his pants around attractive white women. Miss Billie, Bobby's mother, puts a genteel spin on it: "The attempted outrage of four white women upon the island."

The first and second times, Tyrone put his pants back on when the objects of his affection threatened to tell his mother, an elder sister in the church. The third and fourth times, the sheriff came over on the ferry and hauled Tyrone off to jail.

And so we thank Miss Pauline, carry the dishes to her sink, pay our bill, and set out in search of Tyrone, often not easy to find. But on the way, we see something scarcer than ghosts. A deputy sheriff is easing down the road in his patrol car.

There is no law on Daufuskie, excepting laws of God, Time, and Tide. These are laws aplenty for locals, many of whom drive without licenses, without tags, insurance, windshields, or mufflers. They drive on public roads with golf carts, ride upon them with horses, often navigating with one hand, holding a sweating rum and tonic in the other. And when their choice of refreshment begins creeping up on equilibrium and judgement, they drive very slowly with legal impunity. There is little risk involved, except when an errant tree, as they are sometimes wont to do, leaps like a deer into the right-of-way.

Call it Daufuskie Diplomatic Immunity.

Heedless of our hopelessly out-of-date registration, the deputy grins, waves and we grin and wave back. Then we stop at OD's Country Market for supplies for supper. OD—officially *Odas*—is not there. Miss Retta watches the store.

Odas' parents, great admirers of the late Otis Redding, were graduates of Daufuskie's two room school and heirs to a genial indifference to the tyrannies of standard English. And Otis is "Odas" and that's good enough.

I lapse into Gullah and strike up conversation. "Where Odas?"

"He ain't chere."

"He loose, o' he lock-up?"

My question brings immediate and staccato response. "Lock up? Why fo' he be lock up? He ain't done nuffin fo' to be lock up!"

Well, maybe not. But Odas is the current hot topic of island talk. He has very recently eloped with Miss Julie, Little Sam's girlfriend. Miss Julie is round, tattooed and very white.

Little Sam is the island mechanic, short, bandied and extravagantly bearded, the man who can fix anything from lawn mowers to golf carts to outboard motors with salvaged parts, baling wire, and duct tape. Little Sam, natural born outlaw, and great grand nephew of Jesse James, who taunts Yankee tourists with bets about being able to tag crab pot floats at 200 yards with his .44. Little Sam, ex-CIA man, who bailed out of the Challenger just seconds before the explosion. Watch the tape close, he says, and you can see him leave in the extreme right corner of the screen. Little Sam, now sorely aggrieved, has taken to liquor and driving around the island with the .44 on his truck seat.

And there is something else, of course. On the night of the Great Escape— according to Sam—anyway, Miss Julie and Odas had run off cross-water, hot-wired Sam's truck and driven all over three counties.

Not able to get them in the sights of his .44, Sam has done the next best thing: He has turned them in for auto theft.

"Well, I seen de po-leece on the islan'."

There is an expansive and gap-toothed grin. "Oh, dey jus' come to help Miss Julie get her clothes outa Sam house."

"Well, where Odas?"

The Gullah have a great and time honored tactic for deflecting questions from pesky White Folks. They can "gator mout," like Miss Pauline when we tried to find out about conjuring. Or they can profess utter and sincere ignorance. Miss Retta masterfully employs the third option. Like Brer Rabbit leading hounds in a broad circle, she ends the conversation as it has begun.

"He ain' chere."

So, we buy lush vine-ripened tomatoes, cucumbers, a Vidalia sweet onion, a pungent cantaloupe for a breakfast treat. We rattle on down the road until we meet Tyrone, jouncing along in a battered van formerly the property of the Ridgeland Baptist Church.

There is an honored liturgical tradition in these parts. Buy a van, wear it out, give the sad and rusting remains to a less fortunate congregation. Daufuskie's First African Baptist, the sanctified bottom tip of a reverse pyramid, gets considerable decrepit transport. The Deacon drives one, as sometimes do his friends and relations; the further the kin, the less roadworthy the van. Tyrone, maybe kin, maybe not, drives the least desirable specimen.

We flag him down. "Tyrone, you know any ghos' stories?"

There is an instant of surprise, then a broad smile. "You got trouble?"

Another detail. We are staying in a house adjacent to the Cooper River Cemetery, a Gullah burying ground since slave times. The house, formerly the real estate office where Miss Pauline did her magic with fried chicken and okra, was actually on the graveyard, until a coalition of islanders sicced a lawyer on the real estate agents. After considerable legal argument, the judge made them move it, and some say, they did not move it far enough. The house may still stand upon graves from plantation days, markers of local cedar long gone back to Daufuskie dirt.

So Tyrone, genial and black snake skinny, eases over to our truck, takes a look inside, eyeballs Miss Judi and says, "I hep you out."

So we plan a campaign. I will pick up the beer, drive back to the house. Tyrone will run a minor errand, then stop by. I slip the truck into gear and Dave gleefully rubs his palms. His boss, way off in Yankeeland, will be most pleased. We stop at the bar at the Freeport Marina and negotiate a carry-out twelve pack, and retire to the house that may or may not still be on Gullah graves.

We wait for Tyrone, but he does not show. Dave watches the clock, and Yankee to the bone, cannot stand the wait. He suggests another interview. I say, "But, we'll miss Tyrone."

Dave has a sudden inspiration. "Miss Judi can wait on Tyrone. We can go see the Deacon." So we leave her there with her .38 and Tyrone's beer, which she begins to drink to settle her nerves.

The Deacon picks up day trippers at the Freeport dock, drives them around the island in a derelict school bus, regales them with tales of Daufuskie's old days—the scrap iron whiskey, the whore house on the Cooper River, the First African Baptist Church where he delivers long and impromptu spirituals after collecting and publicly counting each Sunday's offering. Surely, he has some stories for us, as well.

The Deacon lives in a family compound at the corner of Haig Point and Church roads, in the heart of the heart of the island. It's well after dark when we pull into his yard and park beneath a spreading oak, its branches festooned with long strings of Spanish moss moving in the seawind, hanging like the beards of the conquistadors.

We knock and Deacon lets us in. There is the Deacon, his wife, his step-daughter, and her two year old daughter. Deacon stands in the hallway, his wife watches TV with distinct disinterest while paging through a back issue of *People* magazine, while his step-daughter works braids into the baby's hair, braids like the patterns in sweet grass baskets, row on row like the sea, still woven on Daufuskie as they are in Sierra Leone way over on the Other Side.

I do the introductions and we shake hands all around, then get to the point. Sort of. "Deke, Dave here is looking for some old stories about the island."

Like Miss Pauline, the Deacon goes gator mout'. But for a different reason. "Well I ain't gone say nothin' less dey's sumptin in it fo' me. Was in it for de deacon, huh?"

Reasonable enough, since the Deacon gets paid for his stories. But Dave, having given me his only check, has to call Yankeeland for authority to cut another. Meanwhile, I continue negotiations. "Well, Deke, since you are up-front about what you want, I'll be up-front about what we want."

"What's that?"

"We want stories about conjure doctors, hags, and plateyes."

The house explodes in whooping, hollering, protestation. The Deacon does a little dance, runs in place. His wife leans over, puts her magazine over her head, begins rocking "Ooh Lawd, ooh Lawd!" like she is being pelted with hailstones. The daughter joins the chorus and the baby starts to wail. Dave and I back out the door, making small talk apologies, promising to get back to them after he hears from his boss.

We find Miss Judi as we left her, but a bit bleary and minus about half of Tyrone's beer. Tyrone did a classic Tyrone no show, so we pile into the truck again and set out in search of him.

Down Haig Point Road again to the south end of the island. Left on Benjie's Point, named for one of the old cotton plantations, where the oaks close in overhead and the road looks like a long ghostly tunnel. Down deep sand ruts, dipping to cross a sweet water creek where the 'gators and moccasins lurk and a man might last ten minutes on foot, up to the high ground on the far side where a cluster of shanties give shelter to Tyrone and his kin—his folks, Mr. Harris and Miss Sadie, plus an entourage of uncles, aunts, cousins, and lesser cousins.

The sand snatches us this way and that and headlights flash wildly on the roadside scrub, the oak, myrtle, palmetto. Miss Judi grabs my arm. "Look out!"

I lock up the brakes and a doe, pale and shimmery and

blind from the lights, picks her way across the ruts, not ten feet in front of our bumper.

Tyrone waits in his yard. "Ghos' doe," he says with utter certainty. "I see um alla time." He is speaking to Miss Judi, still in the truck, while Dave and I lean against fenders. "What you see?"

"Big doe," Miss Judi says.

"No, in de grabe-yaad."

"Nothing."

"You ain' see em? You ain't seen Jake?"

Jake Washington, sage and riverman, dead now three years, a man who could read weather by signs in the sky and predict the run of shrimp and crabs by the phase of the moon. Jake's grave lies two dozen feet from my bedroom window.

"You ain't see um? Jake come through the woods like a ball a fire."

Negative.

"You want to see ghos'?" Tyrone asks Miss Judi. She is not sure. "Get up at quarter to fo'. One always stay behind to call de others back fo day-clean."

Day-clean—broad daylight—is somewhere over Africa right now, racing towards us at a thousand miles an hour. But Africa is already way ahead of the sun, here and now, in this Carolina night, soft, seething, and stuck in time.

Tyrone disappears into the house and comes back with Mr. Harris, bent and wizened, a bit unsteady from the lateness of the hour and his choice of refreshment.

Mr. Harris knees up to the pickup bumper, palms the hood for steadying influence. He leans far back and looks way up through the oak canopy, to the deep and velvet sky and pinprick stars beyond. His eyes roll briefly in his head, then snap down when some connection is made and the first tale comes rolling out of him. The little rabbit that sprinted from grabe-yaad brush and before his sweah-to-Gawd-amighty eyes, grew "mos' big as a hoss."

It's straight Gullah, with some serious scrap iron inflection. Dave and Miss Judi get the gist and about every third word. I render the great and liquid Creole into a running set of questions that encourage the artist while providing rudimentary translation. But I say nothing about the African Trickster Rabbit God, or even his cousin Brer Rabbit. The story has come down the generations and is in his bones and in his blood and in the very breath of his body and I will not foul it with anthropology.

Then there is the ape man, swinging from limbs and wild grape vines, back when Mr. Harris be a'courting, trying to scare him away from Miss Sadie's door. "Thought it was her other man," he confides, "till he swing clean-cross the road."

We stand beneath a spreading oak at the edge of his yard, this music of the ages in our ears. The sea breeze creeps up from the beach, rattles through the palmettos, while Mr. Harris spins tale after tale. Way down in the sweet water swamp, the bull gators offer extensive commentary, like giant, toothy, and skeptical bullfrogs calling out "Believe it? Believe it?"

And we do.

But the spirit is willing and the flesh weak and Mr. Harris reaches the end of breath and equilibrium and inspiration. There is one more story in him, from his days as a Daufuskie moonshiner.

"I go to the still to drap off some barrel," he begins, "load um up in the bully."

On cue, Tyrone's bully swishes around on his tether, fifty feet away, grazing on scant grass and sand, drinking nothing.

Mr. Harris, to foil casual pilferage, has camouflaged the still in the Maryfield Cemetery, where none dare go unless consigning another relative to the power of Daufuskie dirt.

"I turn the bully round, and look an' de grabe-yaad be lit up like day!"

Disapproving Baptist spirits? Exceedingly thirsty ancestors? Mr. Harris does not know. But he knows what he saw. "Like day, man, like day!" He slaps the hood for emphasis. "See every stone, cause they lit up like day!"

"What you do, Mr. Harris?"

"I drap off them barrel."

But Mr. Harris is not the only one who saw what he saw, so he adds, "I don't have to tell that bully to go home!"

I wrestle with the brief vision of that homeward trip. The wide-eyed ox at full gallop, Mr. Harris praying, cursing, clutching for tenuous handhold as the rickety cart slides around corners, leaving a trail of dust in the shadowy moonlight.

"You ever go back there, Mr. Harris?"

"Well, I has to go back, man, my still was there. But let me tell you, I ain' go back after dark!"

And day-clean comes creeping on the eastern sky and suddenly it's Sunday and Dave has to go back to Yankeeland and stand and deliver before his boss who does not know a teaspoon of this dirt is worth more than the entire state of South Carolina and who will eventually decide that Daufuskie is too remote and expensive and obscure and beyond his budget.

But we do not know that now, and we put Dave on the ferry and go home and shower and slick-up and finish just in time for services at the First African Baptist.

It's the island's oldest surviving building, only functioning church, at the corner of School and Church roads, deep in the oak woods, a quarter mile from the two room school where Pat Conroy taught before the Board of Education fired him for insubordination. There are a dozen of us sitting on board benches this lovely Sunday while the breeze plays tag in the mossy tendrils and the cardinals flit and sing like God's little red angels. We are black and white, male and female, "One In Christ" as the Good Book says. Our division being only the two coveys of sisters, knotted up around the strongest voices, so they might do justice to call and response spirituals. Songs like "Jesus on the Mainline" and "Any Way You Fix it, Lord it'll be All Right with Me."

The preacher comes over from Hilton Head on the Melrose ferry. The boat is sometimes punctual, but often not, when the Law of Tide supersedes the Law of Time. This Sunday there is a rare confluence and at precisely 11:00 A.M., the door squeaks open and the pastor strides to the front, climbs into the pulpit and looks out onto his little flock. "The Lord is in His Holy temple," he says in a deep and rich baritone, "and let the redeemed of the Lord say so."

That's our cue to deliver the first of the many "amens" sprinkled throughout the proceedings. But before even the most devout and enthusiastic can get it out, the door opens again. We turn to greet the late arrival and there is the Ram in the Thicket, the Lost Sheep, the one hiding a week in the swamp from the deadly wrath of Little Sam.

It's Odas himself, wearing an immaculate blue suit, broad red tie, and even wider smile.

So instead of amen, there is great and spontaneous shouting—Hallelujah and Praise Gawd and Do Jesus! Odas has got religion, the lost has been found, the last is now first. And we rise and rush to him and embrace him and Odas smiles and we are stuck in time while the sisters dance little quicksteps of joy and the 'gators, for once, don't say a thing.

When the Big Wind Comes

It's mid-September and Hurricane Horace has bounced along the west coast of Florida, skipping along the mangroves, islands, and beaches like a stone. It has finally come ashore somewhere south of Pensacola, and now rumbles and dies over the south Georgia pinewoods.

Out here on Daufuskie the wind is hitting twenty knots and the rain comes in sheets and between the gusts the little waves lap lap along the Cooper River shore and the owls ask questions from the oaks in the old Gullah burying ground.

The wind moans through the Spanish moss, sets the palmettoes rattling like Ezekiel's dry bones, conjuring up nightmares of our fathers' storms, our grandfathers' storms. Stories we heard when the September sky yellowed and the barometer trembled and fell. The Great Storm of Ninety-Three, with twenty foot tidal surge and two thousand dead. The Forty Storm, when neighbors checked on each other by paddling flat-bottomed bateaux up and down the streets of Beaufort.

And then there are the storms we know. Girl's names like they're supposed to be and anyone who knows anything about women would want them to be. Storms like Hazel and Dora and Gracie that made you praise Jesus and hang on while they peeled bark from living pines and blew a thousand beach houses to kindling. Then they named them after men and there was Hugo mauling Charleston and, finally, on down the long and deadly parade to Floyd, which missed us entirely but stampeded two million onto interstates that quickly became the world's longest parking lots.

Locals who traveled two hundred miles in eighteen hours now jockey for space in the island's oldest dwellings, high ground houses that have stood other storms, houses with no pines in their yards, pines which break off twenty feet up and kill you when they come crashing down. Deputy Gunny Barr makes a final sweep of the island, they say, before he heads for higher ground. Hide out till Gunny gets in his boat and you can come out and crack a brew and breeze past the guard shacks and drive around on Haig Point and Melrose Plantations just like you owned them. You can join the hold-outs at Bloody Point, and watch the storm roll in over the Tybee Island Light, feel the surf thunder through the soles of your shoes, and all of you lean at ridiculous angles into the wind, arms outstretched, and not fall, like some tribe of bedraggled Jesuses without crosses.

But we all have our crosses and the official opening of this season of big winds has come, as it sometimes does, about two weeks ago when Miss Nancy took a heavy, blunt object to Capum Billy in the kitchen at Mudbank Mammy's. Capum Billy was down, but not out, and rising from his knees when Miss Nancy ran a magic marker into his right eye. Capum Billy struggled to the phone and dialed 911 and the two hours it took Gunny Barr to get out of bed and to his boat and cross Calibogue Sound was ample time for Miss Nancy's escape.

Miss Nancy is an artist with never-the-same-twice gumbos and Creoles, and works culinary voodoo with sea bass and mullet and blackfish and whatever the skippers of *Top Dog*, *Miss Angie,* or *Sugar Too* sell her when they come looking for fuel money for the next day's trawl. She's got a foghorn voice and eyes like cold blue radar and carbon steel opinions you could not cut with a cold chisel. She is blonde and tan and irrepressible in good humor or bad, passionately berating the kitchen help one instant, then flipping a flounder and sprinting to the dance floor for a quick spin with the boys while the fish sizzles on its other side. But the sea temperature was up and the barometric pressure down and the humidity building, building day upon day, laying upon the island like a wet smothering blanket and her 250 pound pet boar had broken loose and was blocking access to the post office, and maybe she just couldn't help herself.

The EMT's picked Gunny Barr up at the ferry landing and drove him to the fire station where he picked up his squad car, a 1980s vintage Dodge Ramcharger. The truck was idling and the lights were on and Gunny was probably considering fifteen square miles of dark and gatory island and this crazy cast of characters and wondering what the hell to do next when I saw him. I was on my way to beg a bowl of gumbo off Miss Nancy and wondered what the hell the cop was doing on Daufuskie. Later that night, Miss Nancy would get to Capum Billy before Gunny could get to her and they'd patch it up and in a week they would be calling each other darlin' on the phone again.

Capum Larry has seen this all before. Capum Larry is the competition, running the joint down at Freeport, but he bears Miss Nancy scant ill will. "I like her first eighty- seven personalities just fine," he says, which sets him to talking about hurricanes and how the Freeport bar is octagonal to confuse the wind when it tries to get under one corner and peel the roof and how the fracas at Mudbank had distracted attention from a great kicking, screaming, eye-gouging brawl at his joint that same night.

But I was thinking how I loved them both and how Miss Nancy would hug me and feed me when she knew I was hurting and hungry and how I knew Capum Billy was at the helm when I lay in bed at night and listened to the last boat come in and how he played a boat like a musical instrument, leaning far back in the skipper's chair, steering with his foot and keeping one eye on the river like it was Miss Nancy—a beautiful woman about ready to swap moods.

This conversation with Capum Larry about how hurricanes get confused and how people love and hate each other at the same time was a day or two later. That night I was hungry, Miss Nancy was gone and Capum Billy was gone. But the Jamaican girl in the kitchen knew gumbo well enough to get me a bowl and I ate it and drank a Heineken and talked to Mohican, who was bemoaning Blue Tiger, a beautician from Savannah who had stolen his heart and then run off again to the other side.

Mohican calls himself Hawk and he has all the qualities of an osprey, the fish eagle—avian intensity, piercing eyes, and a nose bent beneath too many sucker punches. When he first hit the island, we called him Last of the Mohicans because he shaves the sides of his head and lets the top grow into a long hank that hangs down to his shoulder blades, trailing and flopping wherever he goes like a bit of Manila over the stern of a schooner on a long beat upwind. That name was too clumsy, so we tried calling him Last Of, but there was no rhythm and little satisfaction in it. We tried just Last, but it cried out for another syllable. Then we just gave up and called him Mohican, instead.

Mohican has done time, weeks and months sprinkled through a career that includes raising pit bulls for the ring, dodging the DEA, and once even accidentally shooting his own man in a furious gunfight in the slums of Savannah when a high stakes dogfight prompted the losers to grab iron. He's six three, as big as a Kelvinator, a fugitive from the Law of Averages, at least. And he's Georgia to the bone, cultural heir to convicts turned loose by King George back in 1740 to settle disputed woods between Carolina and Spanish Florida. Mohican is son of a shrimper, grandson of Daufuskie's constable in the old days, back before Gunny Barr when Daufuskie had one full time. He has a good heart and he loves his dogs and his river and his woman, but he is no man to be trifled with.

"Had us a little shout last night," he says, morosely. I had seen the results earlier, Blue Tiger's voluminous bras and postage stamp panties strewn here and there, hanging from the sassafras and crepe myrtle around the back steps, translucent and wonderful and shimmery in the moonlight.

Lonesome and fool for a skirt, I had felt sorry for Blue Tiger. But what a skirt when she wore one. Lithe, blonde, tan, haystack of yellow hair, ready smile and quick and wandering eyes, all smoky with the fires of hell. Mohican had met her two months before. Immediately previous was a passionate and brief affair with a Savannah Beach barmaid. But the barmaid turned up pregnant, and after years of raising other women's kids, Mohican—now forty-odd years old—is determined to finally raise one of his own.

Bucking up like this is rare, noble but not without cost. This latest shout was triggered by Mohican's announcement he would accompany his former lover to her first pre-natal assessment, and he would pay the bill.

So I listen to his woe and remind him of what I should tell myself—that Blue Tiger is not the only girl who has one of those things and that he has to do right by his unborn child and if doing right was easy it would be as common as grass on Daufuskie—not centipede or Kentucky blue, but the contents of hand rolled cigarettes that are easier to come by down here than the morning paper. Like what Mohican has stuck in his pocket; what we share in the rustling palmetto moonshade before I head back to my lonesome shack to find another e-mail from Blue Tiger waiting for me.

There's me and the computer and the spider. The spider came two days after I put Miss Judi on the airplane, and I let it stay. It's a southern banana spider, yellow and spotted like a leopard, and big enough to straddle a good sized coffee mug. Miss Judi is a Minnesota redhead, with eyes like deep green pools that I fell into and was going, going, going down for the third time when I couldn't take her drinking anymore and I put her on Delta 305, with stops in Atlanta and Minneapolis. The spider is strung across a corner of my front porch, so close to the door that you have to watch yourself getting into the house.

Back when I was nine or ten, I got swapped across the face with a spider like that. I was on Daufuskie in the back of a jeep going thirty and there was no windshield and there was this little speck between the trees up ahead and *whop!*—I had a spider as big as my nose upon my nose and swear I could feel spider feet scratching at both ears.

I did not jump out of that jeep and roll in the Daufuskie dirt, but I hated spiders ever since and when I got old enough I used to shoot the really big ones out of trees with a .22. *Fipp!* when I connected and the body evaporated into yellow mist and amino acids and eight legs just quivered and hung there on the web all by themselves. A dozen years later, I laid a micro-dot of LSD upon my tongue in a grungy trailer house outside of Bluffton and there was a doughnut-sized fox spider under the pile of dirty dishes in the sink and later when I got to grinding my teeth and tried to take a shower the bathtub was level full of interlocked hairy spider legs that ran up the wall and covered the Masonite in an endless and horrifying mosaic. Then I was down on Daufuskie and I put Miss Judi on the plane after five years of hopeless love and the spider came to my porch and like a boogered pool shark who shoots a rack of eight balls to settle his nerves, I did not kill it.

Blue Tiger liked voodoo and I had published a book on the old Carolina root doctors: John Domingo, who wore a snake ring of Congo silver and kept his hair tied up in little knots to keep the witches at bay and the whores turned their heads as he passed so he could not mar their beauty; Dr. Bug, who gave a thousand draftees the hippity-hoppity heart; and the Great Dr. Buzzard, the courtroom specialist who for forty years tipped the scales with a wave and a nod and mysterious white powder sprinkled throughout the halls of justice.

I was taking the air off my porch one fine spring morning when the painted buntings were mating and I saw a willowy blonde walking around in the Gullah graveyard with Little Sam. I hailed them and they came over for coffee and the first smoke of the day. That's how I met Blue Tiger—tan, long, lean and me lonesome. She read my book and wove beads and feathers into her hair and wore lace dresses and cowboy boots and the air crackled whenever we stood too close. But she was Mohican's woman until she found out about the Savannah Beach barmaid and then she left the island and Mohican followed and a week later hauled her back and painted Hawk Loves Tiger on his roof in John Deere green.

But between the escape and the sign on the roof, she had asked about my extra bedroom and I said, "I don't know, honey. This island could get pretty damned small." And then I suggested dinner and drinks in New Orleans, instead.

The spider grew and one morning there was another with her, a male, delicate, brown, and no bigger than a dime. They faced each other for a week and then he swung in a wide arch toward her rear end and crept a quarter inch closer each day.

And then the turtles crawled and I met Miss Mary Ann, who walked barefoot on hot coals to put her faith to fiery test.

Miss Cathy brought her onto the island. Miss Cathy walks on fire, too, and they break arrows and bend rebar by putting the ends in that sacred and lovely and deadly little spot right below the larynx and push till the bar bends or the arrow breaks and they never draw blood at all. The women met up in the Alabama highlands while learning such stuff and pretty soon there was a call from Miss Cathy inviting me over for Saturday supper and an introduction.

But I begged off. I had already told Mohican I'd eat with him, and we cracked crab claws and sucked out the meat and drank Tennessee whiskey and talked about women. But you can't beat God's sense of humor and the next morning I walked into the First African Baptist and there was Miss Mary Ann, long-boned, tan and exotic and wearing one of those dresses God grinned when he made summer for.

The preaching was Baptist and good, all about sanctification, justification, and the healing power of the blood of Jesus. And then we joined hands before we left and sang *Amazing Grace*.

But I did not hold hers. That came later. They came for supper and I poured dark rum and fed them curried chicken while the spiders carefully courted. And then we went down to the beach at Bloody Point to watch the moon come up round and gold as a pirate doubloon.

It was a turtle moon, and a quarter mile down the beach I saw the herringbone in the sand and no track leading back to the sea. We followed up through the tidewashed boards, the driftwood, the ricks of last year's spartina, lying in the moonlight like tipped shocks of wheat in a long snowy field.

And we found her, an old loggerhead big as a kitchen table, crusty with barnacles and trailing seaweed, way up near the first pines, weeping great tears for babies she would never see while eggs like greasy ping-pong balls gently plopped into a hole scooped with her hind flippers into the loose dune sand.

"Smell her," Miss Mary Ann said and took my hand. I did and it was sweet and salty as sex on a hot summer afternoon. And then I touched the back of Miss Mary Ann's neck and she turned and smiled and her eyes caught the moonlight and she knew and I knew and I was gone, gone, in love again, gone.

We followed the turtle home to the sea. Struggling and panting, forty yards before collapsing chin down into the sand. She lay for two minutes and rose and plodded off again, but did not make it as far. She was gasping and spent when the first wave hit her and it gave her strength we could not fathom and the last twenty yards were as fast as any turtle could go. We waded into the surf, us and the turtle in the moonlight with the frothing water rolling around all our desires and then we could go no deeper so we whooped and watched her take one last breath of air, then go.

Then Miss Mary Ann went back to Florida and Blue Tiger and Mohican had a shout and he took her back to Savannah and got drunk and fell off the roof trying to paint over Hawk Loves Tiger. Blue Tiger and I were talking on the phone when Mohican stumbled up my steps, red-eyed, bespattered with roofing paint, stuck all over with oak and magnolia leaves.

Blue Tiger wanted to talk and he wanted to talk and I very quickly did not want to talk with either one of them. But he was hurting and I was his friend and she was beautiful and fixing to get me killed so I hung up and poured Mohican a good stiff whiskey.

He drank it and that's when I learned all about the Savannah Beach barmaid and to keep the tale from getting too tiresome, I fetched out a picture of Miss Judi and we commiserated about the intricacies of hopeless love.

But love is what it is, sometimes hopeless, sometimes like the love of a turtle that will come back ten thousand miles to lay on the beach where it first saw the light of day and first dodged gulls and later sharks getting to deep blue safety.

Blue Tiger may have been blue, but she was far from safe.

Mohican brought her back to the island again. He should have known better than to attempt serious discussions in a skiff at twenty knots. The whine of the outboard and the rattle of waves on the hull and always the buffeting of wind about the ears mute all the glorious nuances and female body English is expended just holding on. That reunion lasted as long as it took him to get her ashore.

Mohican left her beneath the spreading oaks at the county landing, where you can see Savannah but cannot get to it without a good boat and carnal knowledge of a dozen miles of tricky channel. Then he went home and called me and said, "Tiger told me you two have been talking on the computer. She told me she can stay at your house anytime she wants. I left her at the dock. You can pick her up whenever you get around to it and you may conclude your business however you please."

That was two months after the turtle crawl and I was cooking for Miss Mary Ann, back again from Florida. I walked onto the back porch with the porta phone and talked while I watched the spiders mate, belly to belly, the male delicately dipping the tip of his abdomen, gently easing into the female's rear cleft, swollen to be the envy of any woman in heat. I invited Mohican over for supper. He hung up. He called back. He hung up again and I ignored the next half dozen calls that came while Miss Mary Ann and I sat and ate gumbo nearly as good as Miss Nancy's.

The next afternoon we were way out on the Bloody Point beach, looking to see if the turtles had hatched. We found a dead deer, nothing but skeleton and skin and skull, half buried in blow sand but we could not find the nest. We turned back to the sea and we saw Mohican's truck coming down the beach at forty and Miss Mary Ann who knew all about this but loved me anyway said, "You're about to get your ass whipped."

Age and honor would not let me run. And way out there on Bloody Point, a mile from tall timber, there was no place to hide. I could not shoot him, even in the leg to give him opportunity to reconsider. My pistol was not only unloaded, but also five miles away, home in my dresser drawer, wrapped in oily rags against the salt air that was forever trying to affix a patina of fine red rust to its fine and deadly blue steel. So I stood there and watched the old Chevy come closer, then closer and then I saw two people in it, sitting so close and tight they looked like one from a distance.

It was Mohican and Blue Tiger, deep in afterglow and in love again. The truck rattled to a stop and Mohican leapt out and strode to where I was standing helpless and empty hand-ed and embraced me and said he loved me and he was sorry. I put my head against his strong shoulder and put my arms around him and grabbed his long hank of hair and said I loved him too and he could cuss me anytime he needed so long as he apologized later. I looked in the cab at Blue Tiger and she was all up in beads and feathers and she looked at me and her eyes were slitted and yellow like a rattler's. "Lost my contacts," she said, "these Halloween ones are the only ones I have." And then she stuck out her tongue at me, all pointy and delicious and she flicked it beyond her teeth like a snake.

Mohican looked at the sad remains of the deer and kicked at it and Blue Tiger got out of the truck and wrenched the head free and looped it into the pickup bed. Later, on the way home, we saw it perched on a fencepost at the corner of their yard. And Mohican had painted Hawk Loves Tiger again, but this time on the east wall of his kitchen.

And when I got home I watched the spider eat her mate but I did not say anything about it to Miss Mary Ann.

So now the hurricane dies and the tide ebbs and the wind bucks the current, galling the Cooper River into five foot swells that set the floating docks plunging and creaking. But the rain has slacked off, and over at Freeport there is a fire and the hardcore have gathered to drink and smoke and try to get laid and cuss one more storm that could not run them off this island. There is Robbie the shrimper, Sparky the electrician whose house just burned from an electrical fire, Turbo the watery Good Samaritan who will hit the river in any kind of weather and drag you home, no matter what. And Lordy, Miss Heather, drunk, nubile and extravagantly tattooed, an off duty female Melrose security guard, a lady lawyer, a real estate speculator, several persons of uncertain sex and occupation, and Mr. Garth, the canned collards king from Columbus, Ohio, down on vacation and caught in a storm and quite happy for it. Capum Larry presides, one hand in his pocket, whiskey in the other, khaki head to toe, looking like a Panama Jack poster and liberally sprinkling witticisms among the assembled.

But Miss Mary Ann is down on a Florida beach just north of Melbourne and is about ready to walk on fire again and I sit and sip my whiskey and stare at the coals and wonder. Capum Larry eases up and asks, "Would Mary Ann walk through that?"

"Flames too high," I say. "It'd set her britches on fire."

Capum Larry grins. "Yeah, she'd let them get down low with a thick layer of insulating ashes."

And then I tell him about the bent rebar and the broken arrows and he does not know what to say so he walks off to talk with Turbo about the bucket of flounder he got with a gig before the storm blew in.

And the drinks come around again and the wind whistles around the eight sided bar and, too confused and too weak to even rattle the tin, dies down to a whisper. Way out in the river a porpoise blows and we hear the great throaty whomp and we know the creeks are full of mullet. If the weather settles, Capum Larry and I promise we will get after them tomorrow.

Rebel Yell

The wind is off the beach tonight, smelling of the sea and the sandy pine ridges and the dark swamps between. It ghosts through the cassena and scrub oak and wax myrtle and sends the acorns rattling down into the saw palmettoes, popping and pinging like wild runs on a jazzman's drum. Out in the high marsh a bull gator grumbles and the sun slides down the copper sky, slipping west towards Savannah, setting distant roofs and steeples ablaze with holy flame.

General Sherman did not torch Savannah but the Lord's burning rage most surely could. The papers are full of it, revelations of the forgotten midair collision back in 1958, the plane that did not make it and the plane that jettisoned its atomic bomb into Wassaw Sound and did. Now the bomb cooks and the experts argue about critical mass and rates of corrosion and I'm thirty miles away, halfway up a slash pine, waiting for a buck, or the end of legal shooting, or a superheated blast of irradiated air.

Daufuskie Island, South Carolina, Game Zone 11. One hour before sunrise to one hour after sunset and no limit on bucks from the middle of August to the first of the year. Call it reverse psychology. Nobody bothers going out during squalls, tornadoes, hurricanes or earthquakes. Few hunt before the first frost slows down the snakes, and only the most foolhardy do battle with the ticks and, especially, the chiggers which can get to your nubbins bad enough to send you to the emergency room.

But there is no emergency room on Daufuskie, no hospital, no doctor. If you're about to die, a helicopter will pick you up on the road in front of the fire station and fly you to Savannah for three thousand bucks. If you fall off a roof, or chain saw your leg, or get snakebit, there is a long boat ride across deep blue water, but the county landing is a mess and you can't get a boat in on anything less than half tide, so you are damn careful.

I'm on the edge of Miss Sally's yard. Miss Sally is off in France, painting and drinking wine and eating cheese and when she left she said sit on my porch one evening and snag you a deer. But Miss Sally has a couple of dogs and they are off at the kennel but the fleas are not and they are lonesome, so I am sitting in a slash pine a hundred yards away instead, watching Miss Sally's stand of winter rye and listening to the acorns dropping into the woods all around.

Miss Sally and I are cousins a couple of times over. Her great-grandmama and my great-granddaddy were first cousins, but they got married anyway. That was after great-granddaddy was turned down for duty on the Hunley. And after the Yankees burned Miss Sally's great-grandmama's plantation and killed her great-granddaddy in the Battle of Honey Hill, where they tried to cut the Charleston and Savannah Railroad and the Rebels stacked them up like cordwood.

We did not know all that when we met, but we figured it out as soon as we got to swapping stories. Now we love each other and call each other cousin and I haul her groceries off the ferry when her truck is broken. And she feeds me the creoles and gumbos and tortes her great-grandmama fed my great-granddaddy and lets me hunt on her land when she is off in France, which is exactly once since I've known her. But if you sit in a slash pine and look at these woods and listen to the acorns plopping into the palmettoes and the ospreys screeching and the gators mumbling, you'll know one time is enough, if one time's all you get.

The glory of just sitting here is one thing, the glory of a fine rifle and a tight stand and the right wind is an abundance beyond imagining—an atomic bomb notwithstanding. The tracks are pegged everywhere into the sandy earth and the half-eaten acorns snapped underfoot like bubble wrap when I eased into the stand an hour earlier.

But "dey snake in de gaaden," as the Gullah say. Biting gnats too small to see and mosquitoes that whine in and out of my ears and the nightmare visions of nuclear firestorms and the somewhat less metaphorical snakes—copperheads and moccasins and diamondbacks—along the bloodtrail I know I will soon have to follow.

So I worry the bolt handle on my six-five Swede with my thumb and forefinger and think about the last time I got a buck in the crosshairs of the old Weaver variable. I was off in Minnesota on a high hill overlooking the lake and the buck was way out in the snowcovered field chasing a doe instead of slipping along down in the prickly ash where he was supposed to be and we ate him all winter when wind rattled the shingles and the snow piled and the frost made swirling Picassos like pheasant feathers on the storm window panes.

I spent the better part of my life up there, where you fish

through the ice and sip peppermint schnapps and sauna naked in mixed company and if you're lucky some woman will beat you with a birch bough until it feels real good when she stops.

I got there by accident. I was on my way to Alaska, but there was a broken truck and thirty years and two wives and a tribe of children raised on fish and grits who learned how to break a horse and skin a deer and cuss in Norwegian and Finn. And when I finally got back on the road again the kids were grown and I was an old man headed back where I came from.

Lay yourself up goods in heaven, the Good Books says, where moth and rust do not corrupt, nor thieves break in and steal. I try to and Lord knows I need to, considering sundry indiscretions and a long string of aggrieved and greatly embittered women. But I am down on Daufuskie Island high in a slash pine tree and out in the blue water an atom bomb is cooking and the moths and rust are corrupting and thieves are breaking in and stealing.

The rust is on the bolt handle, which I touched two weeks before and forgot to wipe afterwards. The sweat and salt air got to working and now it's brown where it used to be bright even though it's smooth now from me worrying it for an hour in the stand.

And moths are corrupting everywhere, on the front beach at Melrose and Haig and Bloody points where there are golf courses and million dollar real estate and you can't go unless you belong. The Yankees and the yachties and the yuppies and the dot com millionaires and the descendants of Gullah slaves and poor white folks getting squeezed out by a long series of felonious swindles.

And now there are plans to dredge an inland marina into the heart of the island and condos and another golf course, so we met on a shrimp boat, me and Miss Sally and Miss Mary Ann and Mr. Bo and his boy, Little Buster. Little Buster looked on while we put our names to paper and raised Dixie cups full of good champagne and his daddy toasted "To the Woods."

We call it the Shrimp Boat Charter and maybe someday Little Buster will be an old man and can say he was there when it all began, when an outlaw band of back-of-the-islanders first dared feed a monkey wrench to the gears of corporate progress. But meanwhile I'm a hero to people who cannot help me and an enemy to those who poison dogs and burn houses and ditch and drain and scalp and sell.

And there is also the atomic bomb and a plague of serpents and bugs, but I'm hunting deer anyway and thinking about the story Mr. Bobby told me when we were out after mullet one windy ebbtide, how the plane blew up and the blue fire shot all around and little pieces of twisted aluminum stuck everywhere in the trees. Mr. Bobby and Miss Emily live a couple of miles through the woods, out by Bloody Point, in a house they built from remains of a pulpwood barge and a railroad trestle, all painfully pried apart and laboriously hauled ashore. Mr. Bobby grew up here and sailed three times across the Atlantic and patched up planes for the CIA in Laos then settled in again, homesteading with Miss Emily back in 1974. It was bacon, beans, and kerosene in those days, and the venison Miss Emily took with her .30-30 while Mr. Bobby stayed home and sharpened the knives. "Boost your woman up in a live oak," he advises. "That way she'll stay there till you come get her."

I have no woman. Not yet, anyway. I'm working on Miss

Mary Ann, but she lives in Florida and enjoys city pleasures and some ignoramus told her venison tastes bad. But then she walks on fire at night gatherings of wounded women, so she might have the grit for the woodsmoke and the snakes and the spiders. She might even learn to throw a cast net and pick oysters and make deviled crab, though I doubt she would ever consent to being left up in a live oak tree when the shadows lengthen and the hoot owls start talking about you way back in the swamp.

I'm in a slash pine, not in a live oak. But there are two of them a hundred yards away, each at least a century old, each six feet thick, crowns shading a half acre of this sandy ground and steadily peppering it with their fruit. They are a symbol of coastal Carolina, a holy and multipurpose gift—air conditioners, awnings, and organic automatic deer feeders all in one. There is a tangle of myrtle and cassena behind me, a typical border along the high marsh, which is all soppy and shining from sweetwater seeps along the bank. It is a perfect and nearly impenetrable escape route for anything Mr. Lee and his boys might bust loose walking around on the Webb Tract.

The Webb Tract is where they want to dig the hole and Mr. Lee works for the man who wants to dig it. There's an image of Mr. Lee lurking somewhere in the brain of every Jewish New York New Age poet, a pungent flowering of Southern Culture Run Amok, a nightmare of the boys who rode with Nathaniel Bedford Forrest, who wept when they could not kill Yankees any more. Mr. Lee is a wild-eyed, bonafide stump-jumper and proud of it, thank you and damn you, if you don't like it. Snake chaps, long knife, a longer mean streak, a hot temper and a vocabulary that would shrink to a series of grunts if you took away his cussing. He sports a bullet hole in one arm from some previous discussion and a gaunt and slack-jawed brother who helps him sometimes and who has his own bullet hole in his stomach from when he did not promptly pay his bills upon the streets of Savannah. Mr. Lee's got a trailer down in the woods and a couple of thousand dollar bloodhounds on chains and a stove up skiff and a red Dodge pickup with glasspacks. He is a good man in his own way. He likes his licker and loves his children and you would be happy to have him at your side in a hatchet fight. He knows when the fish bite and the shrimp run and the big bucks move, and if you can stand talking to him for an hour you will learn a lot if you can sift through the cussing.

The land Mr. Lee watches over is a cathedral of towering green, where the light comes down as through stained glass, through the live oak, magnolia and yellow pine, down and down, falling in a dappled and moving shadow patchwork upon lesser trees. The soil below is studded with ancient Indian camps, where a litter of Stone Age tools from the old deer hunters lies scarcely covered by last year's leaves. There are deer and turkeys and mourning doves and an old Gullah burying ground, decorated with plates and bottles and spoons, last items used by the deceased, ritually broken and placed upon the graves. And this is what they want to dig up.

But deep in my outrage, there is the soft and tenuous slurping and sucking of hooves in wet ground. It comes from the wrong direction, as deer generally do after you've spent considerable time trying to figure out their ways. I slowly swivel hard right and beneath the tangle I see movement, slim brown legs against the mirror of the slick sweetwater seep.

There is no chance for a shot, but there is a gap in the brush not six feet wide and the deer moves toward it, a squish at a time, like it has all the time in the world, which it does not because I know I will kill him when he gets to where I can see him.

I figure to, anyway. But the wind is off the sea and the buck is in the high marsh and I'm right in the middle. If the wind holds to the northeast I will get my shot, but it eddies a bit to the south while my pulse rises like surf in my ears. And then there is a scramble out in the muck and a great snort and the buck is gone.

The gun comes up but the safety is not off and I sweat and cuss, shake and wrestle my pulse back to where it does not make black crowd the edge of my sight. But then there is another noise out in the mud and then a silence like the silence before the bomb goes off and I know it's another deer.

A deer can cover a mile in two and a quarter minutes. A deer can stand in one spot for two and a quarter hours. But these are Miss Sally's deer, formerly tolerant of dogs and comings and goings. There are at least two of them and they are out in the high marsh and they want the acorns, but I am in the way.

So I will not move and the wind will not switch and the bomb will not go off and I will get a shot if I see horns in about an hour when one of them makes a mistake and walks downwind.

I've had deer do that before, walk right into the gun from sheer impatience. So I wait them out while the past comes welling up and rolls over me like a great breaking wave.

It's 1956 and I am aboard the *Pocohontas,* the wheezy old four car ferry plying Skull Creek between Hilton Head and

Buckingham Landing and there is no atomic bomb on the bottom of Wassaw Sound and the island treelines are a solid deep green and there are no houses along the riverbanks, no powerlines overhead. But land is being sold and developers are drawing maps and I am just a kid and can do nothing about it at all.

And soon enough there was a four lane bridge and Sea Pines Plantation and I eventually took a job there, writing advertising—spinning lies about environmental protection and all you Yankees come down and buy a piece of this quick while you still can. The Yankees came and the eagles left and the gators moved into the water hazards and the square mile of nature preserve became a shopping center and two strip malls. And there are forty thousand where I remember two hundred.

But there are still deer where I used to hunt them when we ran them with horses and hounds and shot Smiths and Parkers and Foxes stuffed with double ought. But now they browse on ornamental shrubbery and collide with golf carts and are subject of judicial proceedings. Kill them, or even count them, the question has kept a tribe of lawyers busy these last eighteen months.

But I am on the far side of Calibogue Sound, deep, fast, and wide, and all that seems another world, a bizarre fantasy that others live by choice, and I look up and there is a deer in the gathering shade of the oaks.

I see no horns, but I know him by the way he moves. Then he turns his head and I see the curl and the muzzle flash, but I do not hear the thump or feel the stock jab my shoulder and the buck sprints into the thicket on a mad race with death that he is sure to lose.

I take up the trail to find the limit of light and old eyes. Twenty yards and the blood runs out in a two acre saw palmetto jungle and it's just two damn snakey to be crawling around in the dark. Mr. Bo is a mile away and there's Little Buster who has been pestering for his first hunt and who did not scald his retinas like I did, first on Carolina beaches, then on Minnesota snow. So I knock on their door and they get flashlights and a pump twelve bore with snake busting number eights and we take up the trail once again.

Little Buster spots, Mr. Bo stands with the shotgun on the last blood and I interpret, encourage and keep an eye out for the copperheads. So we leapfrog through the woods until I see the curl of antler in the flashlight, but I let Little Buster sing out "Dead deer!"

We roll him over and I get the knife, but first I take my thumb and poke Little Buster in that soft and debilitating spot just below his sternum. He winces and I tell him to find it on the deer. He does and he will not forget. I cut and Little Buster learns and Mr. Bo and I talk about the bomb. "The dirty bastards," Mr. Bo says, directing his ire at all of them—the Air Force, the developers, all those in between that don't give a damn so long as the bomb does not go off and the beer is cold and the TV works, the moths that gnaw in darkness, the thieves that break in and steal. And way out across the high marsh, the sky fades from pink to purple to beyond human sight and the lights of Savannah come on, one by one.

The Tie that Binds

It was just after New Year's when I got the last of Miss Mary Ann's stuff onto the island. Most all of it, anyway. There was still the tail end of some whirligig lawn ornament, a forty pound concrete yard angel, and an armload of garden tools locked up in the truck parked at the county landing on the other side.

And then things started to get a little shaky around the house, so I decided to leave them there, so I would not have to haul them back off the island if things got worse.

It had been a long trip up from south Florida. She hauled the cats and computer in her car. I pulled a trailer with a bushel of vitamins, eighty seven pairs of shoes, fifty sets of dangly earrings, three dozen jeans that fit her like mouth watering second skin, and a bed with handles on the head-board and a mattress so soft a man would happily lay down and die when she was done with him.

While I was gone, the Mohican tried to burn out Cooter. He poured gas all over the porch and was flicking his Bic when Mr. Robbie showed up unexpectedly.

Mr. Robbie starts his day with scrambled eggs and the bill of his hat down over his eyes like it should be. The hat rotates as the day progresses and the beers go down. By sundown, it's usually pointing dead astern and then it's time to give Mr.

Robbie plenty of room.

Mr. Robbie and the Mohican had the same grandmother—the constable's wife and Daufuskie's best bootlegger—so he grabbed the Mohican and said, "Listen you dumb son-of-a-bitch; it don't matter if we're cousins, or not. I'll put a bullet square between your eyes the next time I see you on Daufuskie." That's the way things get handled over here: to the point and at no expense to the taxpayers.

"OK," the Mohican said, "but you can tell that bastard he owes me five gallons of gas."

Cooter came home and hosed off his porch. The Mohican went back to Savannah and came back a week later and Mr. Lee brought his things out into the middle of the river and threw them into his boat so the Mohican would not get shot getting his britches.

Then Blue Tiger took up with Cooter, full-time. Which is a shame because Cooter is a retired Savannah longshoreman and ought not be giving a young woman money. A shame because the Mohican is another good man drove crazy, who flipped when he had another woman turn up pregnant; the baby girl was premature and nearly died and Blue Tiger did not like it and made his days ever living hell every time he tried to give the other woman a little money to help with his poor sick baby.

Little Angie did not like it either. Any of it. Little Angie is Cooter's baby, the son he never had, small and bowlegged and beautiful and sweet as pie when sober. She can put on spikes and belt and spider right up an oak and prune it with a chainsaw. She can bring a boatload of lumber over from Savannah in four foot seas and never lose a single stick. She can break a horse and skin a deer and she loves her daddy and she grabbed Blue Tiger by the hair and beat her head against the floor while Cooter walked out onto the dock and had a cigarette to get away from all the screaming and thumping.

I was three hours home from Florida when Capum Larry wandered over from Freeport and told me all this. He did not have to tell me about the buzzards. I figured they were back. The Freeport buzzards, damn them, casting shadows over all of us as they ride the high seawind. Two dozen turkey vultures, three feet tall with wings longer than a man can reach, roosting on the tall pines along the Cooper River, evilly watching the tourists get off the ferry, like they were thinking you-all gone be dead meat one of these days.

Capum Larry figures they are Dr. Buzzard's way of keeping an eye on things. Maybe he's right. They float back and forth between here and Savannah and things seem to go entirely to hell whenever they are around. Dr. Buzzard, Capum Larry says, done put the No Money Root on Daufuskie.

The various Dr. Buzzards, slave patriarch through his great-grandson, are widely assumed to be one person, working out of the same St. Helena Island location for 160 years. Got a problem with the law? See the doctor and witnesses will seize up and the prosecutor's case will collapse. Need a lucky number? Five dollars will get you a tip that could get you a grand. That gal won't give you none? Shee-it, boy, get a Dr. Buzzard Follow Me Root and you'll have more women than you know what to do with. Got a man pestering you? Make his head turn-round backwards and he'll walk down the street barking like a dog. Mention Dr. Buzzard outside and people cringe and walk away. Mention it in a house where they can't run and they'll whoop and holler and praise Jesus.

Years ago, I went to see Buzzy, Buzzard III. I had to get a woman off me. He worked up a Shut Mouth Special, bade me carry it in my left shoe, and gave me a chewing root, a little packet in case she came around while the power was building and not yet sufficient for a sorely aggrieved redhead. "Pop it in your mouth and chew," he said.

I unraveled the paper and examined the contents, which looked like the stems in the down to seeds and stems again dilemma. But they did not smell like De Breath of God, Mon. "What is it?" I asked.

Buzzy dismissed my inquiry with the wave of his hand. His fingernails were long like a Mandarin Chinese, to tell the world he did no physical work. "Don't matter what it is, just pop it in your mouth and chew."

I did, but not for a long while, when the Shut Mouth Special was about worn out. That redhead and I were in court again, and for the life of me I cannot remember the exact circumstances. She was up there on the stand and I knew her well enough to know she was building up to a real tear-jerker, so I popped one of the sticks into my mouth and worked it like a toothpick and looked her in the eye and she turned red and stammered and slobbered and was excused by the judge.

Later on, I moved to Daufuskie and got lonesome and Buzzard III was dead and Buzzard IV was new at the practice and this was serious business, so I called Angel instead.

Angel and I were on a book tour together years ago. I signed and sold *Blue Roots,* my book about the various Dr. Buzzards. She read the cards and made more money than I did. Later on, when my publisher began forwarding plaintive letters from the afflicted, I referred the sufferers to Angel.

Angel is third generation and works only for good unless provoked. She got it from her father who got it from Mother Kent, a bearded, black, and female Jesus from the south Georgia pinewoods, who could call up lightning with the clap of her hands. Angel can look in your face and tell you more than you want to know about yourself. She can bring money or love and make rich white women weep and tear their hair and run around town spending money.

"Angel, Angel!"

"Whas wrong, chile?"

"Ain't got no lovin'."

"What happen to that gal?"

She was asking about Miss Judi. I had put her on the plane six months before. "I couldn't stand her drinking no more."

Angel sucked her teeth and clucked. "You drink that licker, too."

"Yessum, I do, but I behave myself."

There was a long pause, then finally, "I'll burn a love candle for you."

She did and pretty soon there was The Frizz, beautiful and pregnant and strung out on that devil-dust cocaine. I was about to call up Angel again and ask if she could do better when I met Janet peddling around the island on her beach bike. And then there was Sara Beth who helped me make a screenplay out of *Blue Roots,* and finally a gal from New Jersey, with tattoos up one side and down the other, whose name I'd remember if I thought about it awhile. It got to where I was writing down arrivals and departures and hoping the woman going off did not see the one coming on when they passed each other at the ferry landing.

And then I met Miss Mary Ann, who walked on fire and bent re-bar with her neck and conversed hourly with God and pretty soon I did not give a damn about the others. She came for the weekend and later on I found a pair of little black panties under the bed and I said OK, Miss Mary Ann, let's see who roots who.

So I tied a knot in the crotch and tucked in a little shell she had picked up on the beach and then a note she had written saying she loved me. I walked over to Freeport and picked up a buzzard feather from beneath a pecan tree and added that for good measure. Then I dressed the whole package with some of Angel's love oil and hung it on my bathroom wall.

I called Angel again. "Angel, Angel!"

"Whas' wrong, chile?"

"Put out that love candle and burn a money one!"

"Ooh, chile!" And I could almost hear her smile.

So she mailed me a Dressed and Blessed Money Come to Me Candle and I let it burn for seven days in the kitchen sink so it would not break loose and set the house on fire. It was in a tall clear tumbler and when the wax melted there were these little silver and green sparkles moving in the melted wax, like money coming down from heaven. Eight days later, I got a check for a story I had written so long before I had forgotten about it. Eleven days after that, a man sent a thousand dollars he owed me.

And then the money seized up and Miss Mary Ann did too. She said I drank too much and I smoked too much and all my friends were spiritual savages because they drank too much and smoked too much and loved Jesus just like I did.

Maybe it was just island fever. Most of the women get it after they start taking the scenery for granted and get to missing the beauty shops and frozen yogurt. But I never had one long enough for it to set in, so I did not know.

I got ornery and asked her why she had her shorts all in a knot and she hollered "Because you got them in a knot on your bathroom wall!" Then she said she was going to throw them in the trash, but I told her it might bring her all kinds of female ailments and she should throw them in the river instead and the ebbtide would carry it out to sea where it would not bother anybody but the porpoises and they are damn fools anyway and if you don't believe it, just watch them making love.

She tucked her head and black fire shot from her eyes and she looked at me like a bitch dog does when you back her in a corner and she gets ready to bite.

Somebody should have slapped a Shut Mouth Special on me right then and saved me a lot of trouble. But they did not and I told her I had already put one beautiful woman on a plane, and I could damn sure put another on a boat.

She asked me for money for the barge and I said I had already spent all of it on meals and gas and tolls on the Florida Turnpike just getting her sorry ass over here and she had to get back to Florida by herself. And she should round up all those love-struck and disappointed men down there and they could bust their backs like I did and then they could argue about who she was going to live with all the way back down I-95. And I would have Angel fire another love candle and by and by another stream of women would come along and I would be happily occupied, even if I were not happy.

But she was beat because she was broke. So she wept and carried boxes around the house for ten days and slept with her cats for ten nights.

And I was beat too and I walked around feeling like a bastard and thinking about Dr. Buzzard and his No Money Root. Me broke and Capum Larry broke and Miss Mary Ann broke and the whole damn island broke, two developers gone down, another treading water, yet another sucking wind. Million dollar lots with no homes on them and three golf courses where you could sleep on any fairway and a gator might wake you but never a golfer.

It had to be Dr. Buzzard. Jake Washington told Capum Larry and Jake Washington would not lie.

Miss Catherine loved Jake. She hauled the high school kids to the landing in her pickup and Jake loaded them into his skiff and hauled them across Calibogue in the early morning dark. "We doing the right thing, Jake?" she would ask when the swells were running five feet. Jake would shake his head. "I ain' know, Mizz Catherine, I ain' know." The kids got wet, but Jake always got them there. "Ain't nobody gone say a bad 'ting 'bout him."

I can't ask Jake, even though we are neighbors. Jake's been dead three years now and his grave is two dozen feet from Miss Mary Ann's bedroom window.

Here the graves face east so the spirits may flyaway home to Africa. Here are graves with pitiful homemade stones, names and dates scratched in wet concrete with a nail. Here are a scattering of veterans stones, back when Gullah soldiers worked in quartermaster and transportation battalions. Here are graves with no stones at all, just sad and oblong depressions beneath a litter of leaves.

But Jake has the only storebought stone in the Cooper River Cemetery. Georgia granite, simply inscribed "The World's Greatest Father."

It faces east, too.

"Oh, you sleepin' next to Jake," Miss Pauline said when Miss Mary Ann said she had the south bedroom.

"He gone bother her?" I asked.

"No," Miss Pauline said, "Jake restin' easy."

But everybody says Jake liked a good joke. He called his life jacket a No Drown Me Mojo and carried a set of loaded dice to fleece the shrimpers and crabbers and the barge deckhands. Nearly toothless, he would gum package after package of Capum Larry's Nabs and Moon Pies, smiling broadly, the crumbs falling onto his shirt, "to tess um case they stale." So when Miss Cathy felt chilly hands around her when she went to unlock the Freeport Bar, she whooped and hollered and figured it was Jake.

It might have been. Jake worked at Freeport for twenty years and if we do what we love in heaven, Jake is cutting grass, misdirecting Yankee tourists, and hauling kids across Calibogue in his skiff in the dark. Maybe sometimes he gets mixed up and flits around Freeport in the half light, looking for those chillun who now go cross-water in a fast and dry forty foot ferry.

I do not know which Dr. Buzzard Jake was talking about. Rule out the first, the African born student of a village shaman, born and died way before Jake. Rule out Buzzard IV, who got into serious hexing about the time Jake died. Though he now draws clients from Nigeria and the West Indies, he probably wasn't up to rooting a whole island at first.

That leaves Buzzard II or Buzzard III, a distinction as important as when you try to sort out which king did what in Europe.

Buzzard III was the man who fixed me up with the Shut Mouth Special. He knew all about developers, since he saw them skulking around St. Helena, buying creekside properties for pittances and turning them into golf courses and condos and throwing the taxes so out of whack that people miles away had to sell out and move to town and live in trailer houses. Maybe he threw the root on just the speculators and the rest of us are simply having a run of bad luck.

But Oh, Lordy, there is Buzzard II. He foiled circuit court proceedings for forty years, saved from death, condemned to the grave, and gave a thousand WWII draftees the hippity-hoppity heart. Buzzard II lived back when development was young gals growing up. Maybe some Daufuskie oysterpicker owed him money and would not pay and he rooted this whole end of the county out of spite.

And that was heavy to consider. So I waited for the buzzards to leave and they did not. I haunted the mailbox but only bills came. But by and by Miss Mary Ann sweetened up a little and let me into her bed once again. It was only once and very early in the morning, but I held her and cried quietly when it was over.

I lay there with the dawn slipping over the pines and shining off the slick Cooper River lowtide. And I turned to the window and there was Jake's grave, iridescent blue in the creeping light.

And I said, "Jake, you old bastard, why don't you tell me something." And Mary Ann stirred in dreams of whatever fire-walkers dream about and her breath was even and sweet upon my face.

And I thought about laying Moon Pies and Nabs on the ground to tempt his spirit. But I did not have any, so I thought how Blue Tiger took Cooter's last loose twenty and disappeared towards Savannah and everybody figured she ran off to join the Mohican again. And of Cooter walking around like his dog had just got run over or his house just burned down, which it did not, thanks to Mr. Robbie.

I thought of all these things while the tide ebbed and began another flood and the barge blew for the landing and I had no money and the buzzards were still there but here in her arms I did not give a damn.

The barge was coming and it would be going and Miss Mary Ann's stuff would not be on it.

Not this day, at least.

And those beautiful little panties were still knotted up, still hanging on my bathroom wall.

A Frail Human Fence

It was a foggy February morning and the tide was slipping toward dead low and the plovers were piping their spring love songs and way off beyond Bloody Point the horns from Savannah bound ships were rattling the windows and testing the lower limits of what we hear.

Miss Mary Ann was in the house burning incense the color of mimosa blossoms and formulated to induce tranquility. I was out on the deck watching the tide and listening to the plovers and the foghorns and smoking a homerolled Bugler. Tranquility a scant commodity those days, I took my Bugler outside, though the house was filled with smoke anyway.

That's when I heard Capum Larry hollering. "Hey, hey! Get your ugly self down to the beach! This frail human fence ain't getting it."

Capum Larry was apt to quote Jimmy Buffett, often outside, but seldom at the top of his lungs. This line was from his song, "The Prince of Tides," about Daufuskie, the island we love.

Back inside, smoke lay like the fog over the Savannah River. Miss Mary Ann was firing up another stick, "I'm heading over to Freeport," I said. She cut her eyes at me, the way a woman does when she thinks you are slipping out for a drink or a smoke of something other than tobacco.

But it was too early for either. I was trying to write and the words weren't coming and I was out having a smoke when I heard Capum Larry holler. Given the choice between finding out what he was up to or sitting there and looking at the screen and breathing tranquility incense that did not seem to be working, I beat feet for Freeport.

I could hardly blame Miss Mary Ann. She had twenty years in the real estate business and then came up here when the market went soft in Florida and figured on marrying a man widely despised by local developers. She passed around her resume and things were looking good before I stood up at the community club meeting and called a man a liar when he said he had permits to build a high-rise condo down at Bloody Point. And then they offered her a job on the beverage cart, instead, where she could earn tips by flirting with golfers and letting them elbow her breasts and pat her marvelous behind.

That's the way it works down here when you butt heads with the big boys. They might poison your dog. They might throw a bag of something under your porch and call the cops and *their* dog. They might throw you off their ferries, fire your relatives, and, for sure, they won't sell you gasoline; pretty soon, if you're not in jail, you'll move to Savannah or starve.

That did not work this time. Maybe it's because I was raised in a house built of Bloody Point bricks.

And that story goes back to another Daufuskie spring day a long, long time ago with the Capum and Old Man Fred Dierks sitting in the shade of the riverbank oaks, swatting gnats, and drinking Dixie Cola and white liquor.

This was not Capum Larry, but Capum Roger, my father. He had just strung wire across the broad salt marsh from

Prichardville, bringing the miracles of light, running water and *I Love Lucy* to a hundred Daufuskie homes. I was eight years old, perched on a pine stump a couple dozen feet away, far enough so the men could cuss, but close enough to hear.

The unmentioned object of this discussion was the Capum's 1946 International flatbed truck, formerly loaded with wire and insulators and now empty, ready for the long barge ride home.

Old Man Dierks was ready to get one over on Lance Burn. Two of the four white men on Daufuskie, Lance and Fred were neighbors, but hardly friends. Lance Burn was magistrate. He kept the sheriff's department radio. He hauled the mail back and forth from Savannah on his freight boat. His wife was postmaster and drove the school bus. And he had the island's only truck, a wheezy Dodge panel wagon

Fred Dierks had a general store and an oyster shucking shed he turned into a beer joint after pollution from Savannah killed the shellfish beds. When the Capum came ashore with that flatbed, Fred Dierks saw a chance to move up in the world.

We called that truck the Rugged But Right. With a flat-head six and no muffler and doors you had to wire shut, she was more rugged than anything else. But no amount of money could have parted the Capum from her.

But bricks could. With a brother, a sister and another on the way, we had just about outgrown the little house and the Capum was stockpiling timbers and paneling and looking for brick. Fred Dierks had a pile of them from the ruins of the Bloody Point big house, built before the Revolution, torn down in 1940 when the ocean was lapping at its front porch. The foundation fell into the sea and Fred Dierks scooped up five thousand bricks and took them to the back of the island where the devil vines and wild grapes took over and pretty soon there was just a long green mound down on the riverbank.

But the Capum saw the bricks peeping through and Fred Dierks saw the flatbed and neither said a word until it was time to go. And then they drank and laughed and called each other names and talked about the weather, the dead oysters, and how the Democrats were ruining the country. And the gnats knocked off and the mosquitoes took over and the tide rose to full brimming flood, the marsh hens cackled, and the river began its long sucking low water slide.

They cut the deal at sundown. The Capum got the bricks. Fred Dierks got the truck, but only after the Capum used her to haul the bricks aboard the barge.

The bricks went to a vacant lot in Beaufort, where they lay among the sassafras and dog fennel. There I learned, then perfected, the fine art of cleaning them with a mason's hammer—blunt on one end, a gracefully curving wedge on the other. The blunt end did battle with fire ants who had taken residency beneath the pile. The other end was for two hundred-year-old mortar. After school for a year or two, a dozen bricks a day. Maybe two.

I will not try and tell you I cleaned all of them. Had I tried, I would be at it yet. I had help. The Capum's rivermen, Dan Williams and Cuffey Dawes, did most of the work, chipping away when the weather was too rough for work on the water.

Between the three of us, we got them cleaned and stacked. Innumerable blisters, a great mound of ancient mortar, dead ants beyond reckoning, and one unlucky copperhead snake, who stuck his head from beneath the pile and set Cuffey to praying and Dan running for an ax. Ten pallets, five hundred bricks on each. The Capum used them to build a house on a high bluff overlooking the Beaufort River, the house in which I grew to a restless manhood.

But back to the Rugged but Right. Daufuskie had two roads, a single intersection deep in the island's middle. Eventually, the inevitable happened. In a great cloud of dust, in a monumental clash of metal, glass, and vocabulary, Daufuskie was snatched from the automotive age.

One truck was hauled to the landing by a team of oxen, the other by mules, both barged to Savannah for extensive repair. Separate trips, since by then, Fred Dierks and Lance Burn were not speaking. And it would be years before either of them spoke to the Capum.

I went north to college, graduated, kept on going, settling finally in far northern Minnesota. I bought land. I married and divorced enough times to know better. Between heartbreak and litigation came a string of delightful daughters, and finally a son. I taught them all to handle horses, boats, guns. And I honored my son with my father's name.

That was all more years ago than I wish to count. Finally, kids grown and scattered, I headed back to Daufuskie where I began working to save what was left of my childhood. There were two paved roads and a stop sign that was still genially ignored. There was a fire station and a microwave tower. There was a golf course at Bloody Point, fairways where wild island ponies once roamed. Fred Dierks was dead and Lance Burn was dead and the Capum was hanging on at ninety-three.

But much of the island was as I remembered—the giant brooding oaks, the winding dirt roads, the sad and careening shacks of the old Gullah rivermen, the cool green woods where the raghorned island bucks dozed away the daylight hours.

But there were plans for more golf and a dredged marina and, of course, beachfront condos, and I joined a group of shrimpers and poets and retired dope runners and we met on a shrimpboat and put our names to papers that said this shall not come to pass.

We scraped up money and hired an archaeologist, and he found Indian bones and developers did not dig their marina. We went online and had one hundred people email the county and stonewalled the condos. But then word got out that Miss Mary Ann was living with me; she lost her job and the money ran out and she would have, too, except she could not get her stuff onto the barge for at least another two weeks and that gave her time to reconsider. So there we were, formerly the most passionate of lovers trying hard to be just friends and it was not working at all.

Bobby Burn says Daufuskie is the only place on earth where nothing normal ever happens. Bobby Burn should know. He's Lance Burn's oldest, an island boy grown up and gone and, just like me, come back here to live. Three times solo across the Atlantic in a sailboat and tenure with Air America, the CIA surrogate in Vietnam, Laos and Cambodia.

Bobby was a ticket agent, of sorts, with the job of bumping distraught passengers from overweight aircraft whenever the Viet Cong overran provincial capitals. And if anybody would know about dope on CIA airplanes Bobby would, and he swears up and down he does not. But he wrote a memoir and donated it to the state museum after he got nervous about having it in the house. Then he took up making pottery and selling it to the tourists.

So if I were to tell Bobby that Capum Larry was in the middle of his yard, peering up into the branches of a pecan tree, and shouting lines from Jimmy Buffett, Bobby Burn would call it just another day on Daufuskie.

But Bobby was on the other side of the island, throwing pots and decorating them with patterns like the Indian shards that show up when the surf thunders and the storm tides slice deep into Bloody Point. And I was out in Capum Larry's pecan grove, both of us looking skyward like we were expecting the Second Coming.

But it was a buzzard, not Jesus, a lone turkey vulture on a bare limb, looking down at us with pointed disinterest. "Didn't you hear what I told you," Capum Larry said, "Get down to the front beach and give us a hand."

The buzzard twisted his head this way and that, raised his wings in a half-hearted flap, then settled again upon the branch.

Capum Larry was talking about the condos. He was talking about Jimmy Buffett. "And the winos surrounded the condos, creating a frail human fence." And he was also speaking of Dr. Buzzard and his curse that no developer would ever make money on Daufuskie.

Some things are hard to figure on this island where nothing normal ever happens. Especially on mornings when the fog lies heavy upon land and sea and the ship horns echo across the Savannah River from Tybee Roads.

Indeed, no developer has made money here yet, and all efforts to turn this place into another Hilton Head have resulted in deserted fairways, unsold real estate, and a long string of bankruptcies. But greed springs eternal and as the other side of the river fills with strip malls and traffic lights and tract housing, a relentless and seemingly endless stream of developers set out to defy history and Dr. Buzzard.

But you don't mess with Dr. Buzzard. In matters of law, luck, or love, there was—and is—no equal. A succession of Dr. Buzzards—African born slave patriarch through his great-great grandson—has been roiling these steamy waters since before anyone remembers, harming and healing, dispensing lucky numbers, provoking seizures in prosecution witnesses, and giving Gullah draftees heart murmers. Speak of Dr. Buzzard outside and people cringe and walk away. Mention him inside and they'll whoop and holler and praise Jesus.

This current plague of developers has proved a tenacious, if inept lot. A thirty-six unit concrete monolith without the input of the local board of architectural review, penthouses in excess of county height restrictions, and a patio and swimming pool upon saline wetlands. They took deposits from potential buyers and closed on two million dollars worth of real estate before their permits were in order.

We did all we could. The emails, the outraged articles in the local press, the calls to politicians. But there was thirty million on the table. Two weeks after we thought we had the project stopped, Capum Larry got a call from a contractor specializing in high-rise construction, looking for marina slips for their crewboats.

So there we were out in the pecan grove, looking up and talking to a buzzard. "Get on," Capum Larry hollered again. "Get on down to the front beach and help us out!"

Finally the buzzard had enough. He hopped skyward a couple of limbs, lifted his wings, caught the sea wind, and soared aloft. We watched him wheel and turn toward the beach and then the fog closed in and we could see him no more. Then Capum Larry grinned at me like he had just won twenty bucks at snooker.

I wasn't ready to go home just yet, so I headed for the beach where I walked south toward Bloody Point while the low tide surf mumbled and the ship horns went ah-oogah, ah-oogah out in the swirling and indifferent white. I walked past the condo site, past an osprey nest, big as a barrel atop a tall pine. I walked past where Miss Mary Ann and I had found the turtle crawl, and I thought of how much I loved her but how I loved this island so much more. I walked way out on the spit of sand that stretches toward Tybee and there in the backwash I found a single brick—red, soft, and oversized—and I knew Old Fred Dierks did not get them all.

And I picked it up and turned and there in the nest was a flash of white and there was a bald eagle sitting where an osprey should have been. And I knew—for a while, at least— we were back on top again.

So I will speak no more of curses, and say nothing at all of miracles. But this is what happened one foggy low tide morning when the plovers were piping their spring love songs and the ship horns echoed across the great Savannah River, on an island where nothing normal ever happens.

Off Sinning at the Temple of Sport

~~~

It's 7:00 A.M. and *The Haig Point Osprey* comes churning upriver from Savannah. Forty feet at the waterline, trim and fast and seaworthy, I can hear the rattle of her Jimmies long before she makes the south end of Rams Horn cut. She is a Breaux Brothers boat, built to haul roughnecks out to the Louisiana oil rigs, but now she makes the county run between Daufuskie and Hilton Head instead. I am on the end of the Freeport Marina dock, watching the dawn creep over the pines, listening to the diesels and the throaty *whomp* of the porpoises as they chase mullet up the sidecreeks. Me and Porgy, my Newfoundland dog, The World's Largest Retriever, waiting for the boat, heading for the Temple of Sport.

I will not be in the First Union African Baptist this Sunday, will not hear the sisters cut loose with "Jesus on the Mainline" and "Any Way You Fix It, Lord." I have told them from the preacher on down I'll be off the island working, which is Gospel Truth because I write for a living. But I did not tell them about the Temple of Sport.

But I wasn't off sinning, unless you count drinking liquor and telling lies and shooting on Sunday. I wasn't heading for a

Bahamian casino or a Biloxi brothel. The Temple of Sport was a gathering place for plantation gentry back when they went after deer and panther and bear and boar with horses and buckshot and hounds. But it's gone now, gone to termites or hurricane or wildfire and nobody seems to know which. But if you are northbound on US 17, just south of Green Pond, South Carolina, look down in the swamps on your left and you might see the historic marker, all grown up in buckbrush and faded and shot full of holes the size of double ought. "On a nearby ridge...a sylvan temple with brick columns built before the Revolution by Barnard Elliott, patriot and sportsman...."

The Temple shows up in *Carolina Sports by Land and Water, including incidents of devil fishing, etc,* a curious collection of anecdotes still in print after one hundred and sixty-odd years. William Elliott, who pegged himself "a hereditary sportsman with my grandfather's tastes and lands" amused himself by harpooning manta rays and being pulled out to sea and by leaping from the saddle onto the backs of wounded deer. William Elliott came here in February of 1843 and found the building gone, the eight brick columns that once supported the roof reduced to two. And now even those pillars are gone, bricks salvaged and hauled eighteen miles downriver to Bennett's Point where they were laid up as a chimney for another house, gone now as well.

But wait. Mr. Charles has found the bricks and set his nephew to cleaning them and hauling them back where they belong. But I'll get to that later on.

This Mr. Charles is the reason I am standing on the end of this dock waiting on *The Haig Point Osprey.* He was sixteen and I was twenty and short a hunting partner and I hauled him out into the saltmarsh and taught him to set blocks and gabble on a single reed and breast out the mallards and blacks and pintails we dropped with our old double guns. And I grew up and grew old and he grew up too, but not quite as old, and I moved clear up to northern Minnesota. But before I left, I gave him a Lefever Nitro Special twenty bore for his high school graduation and reminded him one last time not to shoot where the ducks are, but where they will be when the shot gets there.

I took up writing and wore the keys off three laptops, and Mr. Charles made good as a policy man and bought part of the agency and four hundred acres of ricefields, pine woods, and tupelo swamp besides—the land on which the Temple of Sport once stood. I wrote and whittled away worldly possessions until about all I had left was a long string of publishing credits, an armload of good old guns, and a spread of the finest hand carved cork blocks, pintails, mallards, and a scattering of divers, and a Parson's duck call that I had not taken apart since I taught Young Charles to blow it. And now I am back, living on Daufuskie Island and heading off to hunt with a man I have not seen in thirty years.

And then there is Capum Ed, quail and dovehunter, career navy man, who came up to shoot Minnesota ringbills and went back south with duck fever and bought a vintage Alumacraft, a roll of burlap, and a case of aerosol camo paint and built something that looks like a piece of floating cattail bog. Capum Ed called Mr. Charles and they shot woodies and teal and a few ringbills and laughed and told lies about me and hatched a plot to get me up to the Temple of Sport.

Back on Daufuskie, the skipper eases the throttle and the mate swings fenders over the side and I take a line and snug it off on an uptide cleat. And both of them look at me and The World's Largest Retriever and the cases of decoys and wonder what I am up to, since the only ducks around here are the thousand bird rafts of scaup in deep saltwater that nobody messes with because they eat minnows and taste like anchovies. So I tell them about the blackwater Combahee, the Ashepoo, and the Edisto and the great swamps they drain, the ancient ricefields and the great brooding oaks and the ducks I hope to find and the snakes and gators I hope I do not as they struggle my gear onto the aft deck. And then we cast off and they throttle up and the engines make casual conversation impossible.

Across blue and rolling Calibogue Sound, where the sea ducks wheel and settle in great rafts off Bloody Point, up Skull Creek while the sunrise turns the world conch shell pink and the sea fog tangles all gray and heavy and ropey in the distant cool green woods. In an hour I am loaded into the old truck that brought me and my scant goods back from the far north, and I head north once again, but this time fifty miles and not twenty-five hundred. I drive and Porgy wags his tail and whines and slobbers over the seatback and we watch the country change from saltmarsh to brackish and, finally, to the blackwater rivers that drain a half million acres of tupelo, gum, and cypress bottomland.

It's the fabulous ACE Basin, named for the Ashepoo, Combahee, and Edisto, the rivers that drain it, and the swamps you dream about even if you have never seen them. The miles of rice dikes, sinuous creeks, the straightline canals, the great cypress festooned with moss, the waving cattails, the slick banks where the gators slide to deepwater safety, the swirl and splash of giant garfish and mallards and pintails like distant smoke and woodies in twos and threes pinwheeling into potholes way back in the timber.

We meet at the New Temple of Sport, not far from the site of the old one, a dirtfloor tractor shed making a gradual transition to a fine hunting lodge. Mr. Charles and I, standing in the yard, oaks on one side, pines on the other and thirty years in between. We shake hands and there is a flash of awkward silence that might ask why in the hell did you go off and leave me to hunt the salt marsh all by myself. But that only lasts until we start pawing over decoys and guns. Suddenly, it does not seem so long ago—the palmetto frond blind rustling in the seawind and young me and Young Charles waiting on the birds in the creeping pewter daybreak while the little waves lap lap on our blocks and the owls talk about us back in the cedar hummocks.

But we are here and now at the Temple of Sport and Mr. Charles says "Come on in, Rog, come on in."

We step across a sidewalk of old Temple of Sport bricks. They are big and soft and red and maybe came over from England, ballast in the bottom of a sailing ship. Mr. Charles grins. "We try and drink a toast on them at least once a year."

"Tonight?"

"Maybe. We got chores to do first."

Mr. Charles' chores consists of a walk for woodcock with a shotgun. And mine—setting the blocks and repairing the blind. So he takes off with nephew Young Paul, recently back from cleaning and stacking more bricks, and his buddy Mr.

Pooge, master of Lowcountry cooking—artist with rice steamers, black iron skillets, deep pots with tight lids for oysters, crab, and shrimp. I take off with Capum Ed, jouncing down a road atop an ancient rice dike, where we find two boats—bubba boats we call them—glorified aluminum shoeboxes, one too big and the other too small. We wrestle the smaller to the water and order the World's Largest Retriever to remain on the bank, which he does until we are a hundred feet from shore.

Then there is a mighty splash and Porgy has his front paws over the gunnel and is hell-bent coming aboard when Capum Ed utters a solemn assessment. "Damn, that dog is going to drown us."

The second boat works better and Porgy, otherwise sure gatorbait, rides along in style.

The blind is a mess, but we patch it with brush and burlap and a staple gun, then turn to the decoys, fine corks carved by Jon Skow of Minnesota, a considerable portion of my assets, almost too pretty to get wet. A preening pintail drake, a decidedly disinterested hen, highhead pintail drakes, lowhead mallards, a pair of redheads for the end of the string, each meticulously painted and signed and dated like the fine art they are. But there are strings on them with anchors on the end and Jon Skow calls them working birds, so over the side they go.

Daybreak finds us in the blind again. "I ain't gonna shoot that gun," Capum Ed says when I hand him a field grade Ithaca twelve and a handful of bismuth fours.

"Why not?"

"I'd feel bad missing with shells that cost so damn much."

"Well, don't miss, then."

But he still refuses and sticks to his Model 12 three inch Heavy Duck Gun, a half pound more than it ought to be from the lead Winchester poured into the buttstock. So the Ithaca stands in the corner and I uncase my L. C. Smith as the wood ducks start whistling up the dawn.

Capum Ed noses the Ithaca and whispers, "How come you're shooting the Smith?"

"Can't hit a thing with the Ithaca."

He chuckles. "You reckon it would do me good to miss?"

"Naw. Stock's too short. Too much drop. Figured it'd fit a sawed off, long necked feller like yourself."

We continue the muted character assassination until the first flock rockets in over Mr. Charles and Mr. Pooge with a noise like ripping canvas. "Ringbills," the Capum whispers. Three shots and one bird falls and the flock circles round the far end of the pond, careens off the treeline, then roars in like incoming artillery, from right to left, a shot I seldom miss.

We eat well that night, Mr. Pooge's famous gumbo—sausage and onions and home-canned tomatoes over white rice. Then there are fresh biscuits and nine marinated duck breasts—nine minutes in hot peanut oil over a propane burner in the yard. And the stories go around while we chew—the nest of moccasins dug out of a pine stump, the big tom turkey in the old Black graveyard, and the Lefever Nitro Special I gave Young Charles for graduation, how burglars broke in and took it—everything but the extractor which had worked loose and fallen overboard on its last hunt in the saltmarsh. And I mourn the loss of the gun and the whiskey comes around and we wobble off to bed and the next morning Capum Ed and I are out on the Combahee in a fog so thick you could whittle off a piece and stir your coffee with it.

It swirls and eddies and we can't see a damn thing so we think about snags and deadheads which can hole your boat, brushpiles which can swipe you overboard before you could even get out a good cuss. And the gators that will get you after a snag or a deadhead or a brushpile does. We hear them off in the swamps, grumbling like gigantic toothy bullfrogs.

There is also the matter of King's Grants, back before the Revolution, which gave some of the plantations land to the low water mark, putting the marsh off limits. Then there are the unbroken dikes which you cannot cross, and rules on how long one has to be broken before you can, until you think you might leave your lab at home and bring your lawyer instead.

We blubber along with the current, pondering all these things, trying to poke holes in the fog with two Q-Beams, but the light comes washing back over us and we are worse off with the light. Finally, Capum Ed turns them off and we ease to the side of the stream, finding our way by the running lights' reflection off the marsh, barely visible but not more than five yards away.

We are looking for The Spot, a hole in the south dike, with a good dike beyond. Public water adjacent to a plantation rice field. If we find it and they shoot the field, the mallards will pour in on top of us. Capum Ed mumbles and squints "Too far," he says, "too far." But in another minute we are there and Capum Ed kills the outboard and we ease silently back and forth on the trolling motor and those beautiful corks go overboard again.

But the plantation guns are silent and the fog settles in and the mallards would have just paddled away even if they would have shot at them. So we hunker in the boat, pass the thermos back and forth and smoke home rolled cigarettes and tell stories about Mr. Charles back when he was Young Charles.

We drink more coffee and no birds come. We eat sandwiches, lay them out in full view, and no birds come. Finally, the coffee catching up with us, Capum Ed suggests the final test. We relieve ourselves over the downwind gunnel and when no birds come, he judges the situation hopeless.

"Better pull the blocks and go," he says.

"I could have just as well gone to church," I venture.

I do not know this yet, but I will soon enough. Back on Daufuskie someone got wind of what I was really up to and when the preacher said something about Brother Pinckney being off the island working, somebody stood up and said, "He's not working, he's shooting ducks." And when I get back on Monday I will see the deacon who will ask me where I was and wait for me to lie.

And I will explain and he will roll his eyes because Baptists think shooting on the Sabbath is just about as bad as working, and later he will whisper to the preacher and the preacher will stand there in the pulpit and look at me over his glasses and ask me again in the presence of the assembled faithful.

I do not know any of this, but I have one of those creeping feelings and I tell it to Capum Ed, who finishes the wrap on a pintail hen and cuts me a sideways grin and says "Well, at least you can tell them you were at a temple."

And I say "Ok, Capum, I'll do just that."

Somewhere back in the swamp a bull gator grumbles and a wood duck calls *who-weet, who-weet,* and the Combahee murmurs and seeks the sea.

Good Sign

They call her Polly Mule. "She's bulletproof," Miss Peggi says, "you can shoot from the saddle and she won't even blink. That's a push-button mule, boy. She'll take you anywhere you want to go."

I want to go upwind, off into the clearcut, where the pig sign lies thick among the dog fennel and the crumpled wax myrtle and busted down water oak brush. I can see tracks and rooting noseprints everywhere in the dark pungo mud. Polly Mule eyes the territory and lays back one ear.

We are on Delta Plantation, twelve hundred acres of southernmost South Carolina, where the turgid waters of the great Savannah River spread and slow as they meet the sea. There is Miss Peggi, attorney from Georgia Legal Services, Miss Tracy, CPA; lovely women, both. They ride a quarter horse and a paint; me, Polly Mule.

There are deer in these woods, these brooding swamps, out in these ricefields, abandoned after General Sherman's bummers rode through the country shouting "All you Negroes is free!" There are quail and turkeys and also bear and panther and a mystery critter you sometimes see at twilight that gives you a long, evil, and yellow-eyed look before loping off into the shadows like a hyena.

Deer season closed two months before, the quail are scattered and few, and you would likely go to jail for bothering the bear and, for sure, the panther and, maybe, the mystery critter, too. You can't take a turkey with anything but a shotgun, and I did not bring one, though I should have, so we will stick with the wild hogs, instead.

Our recipe for wild hog would make Julia Child quit speaking French. You can cook him on hickory for a day and a half, keep him wet with Maurice Bessinger's Honey Mustard Piggy Park Barbeque Sauce, banned now from polite supermarkets for the Confederate flag on the label. You can slice him thin and serve him on rice with more Maurice's, with collards boiled in beer and salt sowbelly on the side. You can save the scraps and mix him with your venison and make ring sausage that would make Jeb Stuart rise from the grave and smack his lips.

Cook him as you will, the genetic recipe would surely please Charles Darwin. Take DNA from the pigs of Spanish explorers, stir in escapees from colonial plantations, add a dash of Russian boar turned loose by high-rolling Yankee swells. Mix well in a large swamp and bake at one hundred degrees for a century or so and you get something more like a werewolf than a farmyard pig, your absolute equal in a ham chewing contest—his or yours.

I could tell you a story now about my buddy Gibbes McDowell, who took his twelve year old boy out and the boy broke a big hog down with his last shot but did not kill it. And how Gibbes jumped in with his knife and grabbed the pig and the pig grabbed back and they went round and round in the pungo mud. When it was over, the pig was dead and Gibbes' hind end looked like a double pepperoni pizza.

I would tell you this, but then I would get off track and have to tell you about the rattlesnakes the pigs eat and the gators that eat the pigs, the sea wind scouring the copper sky and Savannah rumbling off in the bright morning distance like some great growly beast waking up.

Or we could crawl up on a hummock and gather up some fat lighter and palmetto fronds and get us a fire going and pull up a couple of stumps and grab some catfish off the trotlines and pass around the brown licker and I could tell you all of it while Orion wheeled overhead and the fish sizzled and dripped grease into the coals. And you would listen while the night herons cried and the tide changed and a bull gator bellowed like an old fifteen horse outboard that would not quite start. And then the dawn would come creeping and you would know all of it and forever hold it in your heart like I do. But magazines have deadlines and word counts, so I must lay out the words like each one cost me money instead of the other way around or I'd be forever stuck in time on the back of a mule and never get to the rest of the story, to the adventure waiting out in the clearcut and beyond.

"Hey, come on down," Miss Peggi said over the phone. "We see pigs most ever-day. Ride with us and bring a gun." So I packed up my snake boots and skinning knives, my longbarrel Ruger and jumped on the next ferry leaving Daufuskie, the island where I live.

It was a good time to leave. There is a whole bunch to tell you now, and I don't quite know where to begin. I told you about meeting Miss Mary Ann at the First African Baptist Church and about our first date in the July moonlight and finding a loggerhead turtle laying her eggs upon the beach.

About the love we made. Did I tell you about her coming up from Florida and getting all her stuff packed into the extra bedroom and all the good intentions becoming a freeway to hell when she began taking the scenery for granted and got to missing yoga and yogurt? How she steamed and I fried and how she would not eat pork at all and wanted me to make hoppin' john without hamhocks and expected me to serve it on brown basmati rice. And the first discussions that ended with tennis shoes bouncing off the walls later ended with flying books and increasingly heavier objects and then she had a choice between a maple cutting board and a fourteen inch Green River knife and she threw the board, thank God. And I said, "Honey, I am going pig hunting on a mule with Peggi and Tracy and be gone when I get back."

By boat across the blue and rolling Calibogue, up Skull Creek to the county dock, in the truck west on 278, then south toward Savannah on two lane asphalt winding through the tupelos like a black snake. The whole way, I watched for sign like an Indian.

Sign can be anything from a soaring eagle or copulating frogs. It will tell you what you need to know. Something from which you draw determination, or something to send you flat-footed back to the wickiup. I saw my sign a dozen miles from the ferry landing—wonderfully brown and flop-eared and long-snooted and greasy in the morning sun, rooting up the ditch alongside state route 170.

I briefly thought how I might take him. Pull off in the next approach, slip out into the swamp, push him away from the road and maybe get a shot as he ring-tailed it through the gum and cypress and soft maple, all budded up now and red and beautiful in the spring. But I will not Arkansas a pig alongside a public road anymore, will not wait on a log truck's jakebrake for the final stalk. I will do it right. I will ride one down and shoot it with a pistol from the back of a mule or I will not shoot one at all. And this is all good sign.

So that's what I'm doing sitting here in an English saddle on the back of Polly Mule. Looking at sign. Pig sign. Everywhere. Off through the tangled bust-down from when they dropped the big pines, mule hooves slurping along, me reading the earth, heading upwind, one hand on the reins, the other on the butt of the Blackhawk.

Damn, it's a good pistol. Worn but tight and fine and deadly and it shoots where you point it and it will not go off if you drop it on the ground. I have taken deer with it and carried it way up north in the bear woods where a man doesn't go without it, where they lay in the brush and grunt at you as you pass by. But now I am back in the land of my birth and oh what a fine thing it would be to come up on a hog who would not smell us and could not see us and would feel the vibration of Polly Mule's gait and think it just another four-footed herbivore. And I will fetch the Ruger from the holster and in one smooth sweep come down on my target while I haul the hammer back and I will pull the trigger and not think and the gun will roar and buck and rise and I will bring it back down again with the hammer cocked and take a finishing shot if I need one. And the mule will not jump or buck or throw me flat on my back in the middle of the bushes and the other pigs, sorely aggrieved and bent on revenge. Or if the mule gets spooky around the hogs I can always turn her crossways and slip off her far side and use the saddle for a rest and let her run if she wants to and take my chances on the ground, on my feet, with my left eye sharp and shining in the sight notch and me not lying knocked cold as a wedge upon a pile of dead sassafras saplings, where the pigs would leave nothing but my backbone and my jeans and maybe my gunbelt and root my fine Ruger off into the leaves where someone might find it a hundred years from now.

So I ride through the swampy clearcut where I see no pigs, up into the pine thicket with saw palmetto understory, which is perfect for hog siestas, but I still see no pigs. A mile, or more, with the fronds rattling against the stirrups and Polly Mule twitching and cocking her ears and nosing the wind like a bird dog that knows what we're after. Miss Peggi and Miss Tracy await back on the road that runs along the rice dike and I can hear Miss Peggi talk to her paint, trying to quiet her because she wants to be off in the thicket with Polly Mule, but Miss Peggi is worried about footing out in mud like chocolate pudding.

I work my way though the pines always upwind until I break out onto the broad high marsh and I see the rooftops of Savannah off in the distance, golden in the afternoon sun and the Talmadge Bridge shining like some great silver heron, its wings spanning the river.

Then Polly Mule is sinking past her hocks and I can go no further, so I turn and ride along the shore, cross the gator wallows and otter slides until I see the great green jumble of points and hummocks of Daufuskie to the east and I wonder about Miss Mary Ann, and I choke back the great urge to turn the mule and get in the truck and take the ferry and be with her while she is hurting. To hold her and lay with her and feel her sweet breath upon my neck and hope to hell she does not reach for the knife next time. But mules and pigs are safer than a woman scorned, so I work my way back into the pines, downwind now, and I know I will see no pigs.

Your woman may lie to you. So may your best friend, your preacher, your senator. But your mule will always tell you the truth, though you may not like to hear it. And Polly Mule tells me she is about to dump my carcass onto the ground. First her ears, one back at 45 degrees, the other further, the rolling white in her eyes and then the muscles along her back, tightening, tightening like a giant spring. I could feel it through my saddle, my English saddle, that slippery flat-seated friend of tort attorneys everywhere, that heinous contraption that has killed more Englishmen than the Falkland Islands War. Give me a western saddle with a horn to hang on to. Give me an Australian saddle with high cantle and deep seat. Give me anything else and I can stay on top. But the saddle is Peggi's and it's English and I'm a goner.

But I'll give Polly Mule credit. She waits until we are out of the clearcut, where the stumps and stobs and cypress knees rise out of the earth like punjis. She waits until she has me back out on the road.

There is time for one brief expletive and time for wishing it were a prayer instead. But the ground comes up fast and I hit it with the small of my back and the pink fire shoots all around, but I do not hear any bones break and Sweet Jesus I am still alive.

I am looking up and Polly Mule is looking down giving me the evil eye, but I still have the reins and say, "Damn you, the only way I will turn you loose is if you step on me first."

And she does not, so I roll over and grab her by the leg and haul myself to my feet while the woods and sky wheel around in a giddy kaleidoscope of greens and blues and glory.

Miss Peggi and Miss Tracy round a corner at a quick trot, then pull up short when they see me hanging on the saddle.

"We figured you were about to shoot," they say later when they have me in the truck heading across the Talmadge Bridge. "You got insurance?"

"No."

"You want to go to the hospital?"

"No."

"You all right?"

"No."

I had climbed back onto Polly Mule and had ridden another hour and had seen no pigs. She had tried to throw me again, but I had seen it coming and had slipped out of the saddle and walked her until she changed her mind. The walk was good and so was untacking her, brushing her down and picking the pungo from her hooves. I hurt from head to heels, and in a couple of days my backside would look like a pig had gotten ahold of it. But right then the moving was good and it kept me thinking about the hole in my heart.

Now we are high above the river and the ricefields stretch out like checkerboards of browns and other browns and the canals glisten like strips of cold rolled steel. Daufuskie lays off to the east and through the water in my eyes looks like a fine green smudge along the edge of the world.

Savannah awaits, and a dinner party where the hostess, blonde and round and wonderful, will meet me at the door and take my hand and say, "Roger Pinckney, we have something in common."

And I will hobble inside and grin and say, "Yes ma'am" and ask if we are somehow cousins.

And she will laugh and tell me we have both been thrown by the same mule.

And I will holler at Miss Peggi who will be most emphatic that my hostess was not thrown, but simply fell off.

And the red wine will come around and later on my hostess will find me in the kitchen and take my hand again and tell me how happy she is that we have met.

But that is all to come, as we roll down the southern end of the Talmadge Bridge, and I look out over Savannah, looking for good sign.

Gatorbait

It was a Monday in May and way too early for a drink. But a gator had just made a snatch at Phil the Bug Man and he needed one real bad. So I put up the iced tea and got out the jug and poured him a dram and we sat out on the porch and watched the boats on the Intracoastal while he told me all about it.

He was fishing one of the Melrose ponds, off the end of the little dock where they scraped out dirt to drain the swamp and make the thirteenth tee. There are bucketmouth bass in there, hog cats, too, and slab bream beyond count. You can't eat them from the pesticides and herbicides and God-knows-what-all they spray on the golf course, but if you're happy with a twitching rod and a howling drag, you'll love fishing the Melrose ponds on a hot still day when it looks like rain but it doesn't.

Phil the Bug Man is from East Tennessee and he knows his bass and the poppers and divers and spinners that drive them crazy. He caught and turned loose a couple of nice fish when he noticed a three foot gator easing to the dock, attracted by the action. Phil sent it on its way with the butt of his rod.

There was time for one more cast. Then the water before him erupted in a frenzy of white and green and brown and a twelve foot gator lunged upon the end of the dock. There was an eternity of tooth and white maw as the gator scrabbled for toe hold, then lost it, and disappeared underwater in a great sucking swirl.

Phil was struggling with pulse and sphincter when he caught movement to his left. The gator was easing up the bank, trying to get between him and his truck.

Now this Phil the Bug Man is a man like me. He likes women and licker and other stuff, too, but he sits beside me in the First African Baptist and when he looks you in the eye, you know he will tell the truth.

And Phil has punched Hell's Own Time Clock. Crawling beneath houses spraying stuff you would not want near you, for more bugs than you can name, dodging copperheads and praying the brown recluse and black widows won't bite. And before that, married and divorced maybe a couple of times with some wild-ass Tennessee kids in the bargain. And even before that three times shot up in Vietnam and finally transferred to Korea where he started a firefight with his Browning 50 along the DMZ when he smelled Chinese and the dark did not move to suit him.

But this gator had him boogered good. Two hours later, the whiskey shimmered in his glass when he talked about it. I poured another shot to replace what he spilled.

We swapped gator stories while the river rose to brimming flood, and the sun eased off toward Savannah and the marsh hens cackled when the tide switched directions.

I told him about the bull gator that came at me while I was hunting wild hogs in the salt marsh. How it first grumbled and then roared and I saw the marsh move before its snout like the wake from an incoming torpedo. And how he sheared off at the last second and I might have shot him at four feet I but could not even see my knees, much less the gator.

He told me about the Rottweiler running home from the beach with Caleb and Little Jennifer and how the dog took a short cut across a pond and disappeared like an eighty pound Hula Popper. And about the man who tipped his riding mower into the same pond a month later and by the time he got untangled from the machinery, the machinery was the least of his worries.

I told him how Ray and Dennis got lickered up one Saturday and got their deer rifles and thinned out a few of them and the game warden came and read them the riot act but made no arrests.

We spoke of this and more, but not of the swamps, drained now into water hazards, the gators following the water and their digital brains twenty years reprogramming prey from coons and deer to pets and people, this great unscrambling of ten thousand years of natural history and the harvest reaped when you try to get money from the earth without first planting seed. We knew this sorry equation, but did not speak of it. But I saw it in his eyes, in the wrinkles at the edges of his eyes, as Phil the Bug Man looked out upon the river.

We did not speak of the ancient oaks, standing here and there amongst the second growth pines, oaks that saw slavery and piracy and war, oaks you want to embrace and beg for stories. We did not speak of the shell middens, piled high in the woods where ancient Indians opened oysters. We did not speak of the sad and careening shanties, where the woods once rang with the music of Gullah, the gentle patois of slave ship, blues, and voodoo, shanties empty and sinking back to the earth from whence they came. And of the Gullah rivermen, starved out after pollution killed the shellfish beds back in 1956, and how they moved to Savannah and found work in the same industries that had driven them from their island home. So we swapped gator stories instead, me and this Phil the Bug Man.

Phil had left his rod on the dock, beat the gator to the truck. Now, his world was shrinking. He would never fish those ponds again. And Mr. Lee had already thrown him off the Webb Tract.

The Webb Tract is an old cotton plantation, six hundred acres of oaks, pines and saw palmetto along the Cooper River, a broad blue estuary separating Daufuskie from the rest of the continent. Mr. Lee takes care of the place, cutting fire lanes, cleaning ditches and culverts, and beating back the ever-encroaching brush with his bush-hog mower. Buddy up to Mr. Lee and you'll get a crack at wild turkeys and have the best deer hunting on Daufuskie.

But the Webb Tract will soon be the biggest marina on the East Coast if Pete and Charles get their way. Pete is an upcountry investor, and if he has a soul at all it is not here with these great mournful oaks, this murmuring river, these marshes that stretch away into the sea haze and change from green to gold with the seasons and the ever-shifting light. Charles is front man, speculator and dreamer, with visions of a dredged harbor, dry-stack boat barns, waterfront condominiums, and another eighteen holes of golf.

We called the state, we called the Feds and pretty soon we had Pete and Charles so tangled up it would take years to work through the snarl. Then I got a letter from a slick Charleston lawyer, liberally sprinkled with Latin, informing me of sundry offenses against Pete and Charles. I was making exaggerated claims of archeological finds. I had interfered with his clients' relationship with permitting agencies. I was damaging their business reputation, impairing their ability to raise funding, and so forth and so on.

I was mighty pleased until I got to the last paragraph. Forever more and from henceforth so-help-me-God, I was prohibited entry upon property owned by Plantation Land Properties, LLP.

Globally, the math did not look so bad. I could not venture upon Iraqi, Cuban, Iranian, and Libyan real estate, nor most of Afghanistan. But figured locally, the numbers were crushing. The Webb Tract and adjoining Oak Ridge, a broad green stripe stretching from soggy creek to shining sea, were fully one fifth of Daufuskie Island.

Then I asked Phil if he would join us and he did and he got thrown off too.

There would be a turkey season the following spring and he would have to sit it out. No longer could he wait beneath the old oak by the Gullah burying ground and look down what he calls Old Ninety-five, the beeline that used to be Haig Point Road, before they moved it so it would not bisect what might be the next gated community, where you can't go unless you belong. He told me of a shot he made there once, a buck at an even thousand paces with a hundred grainer in his .243. Phil called it a thousand meters and you can call it luck, but you know it was not a lie.

So there we were on my front porch, native son and

adopted son, speaking of gators and watching the boats work their way north from Lauderdale, Abaco, and the sunny islands beyond.

Then Phil cut his eyes at me and suggested we take a little tour. So we jumped into his truck and headed down past Cooper River Landing, to the new Haig Point Road, past the Webb Tract to Oak Ridge and there Phil the Bug Man hung a sharp left.

"Damnit, Phil," I said, "you're going to get us busted."

"Hell, Rog, they'll have to stop us first."

I reached for the door handle. Phil stepped on the gas. The woods blurred up as they flashed by. "No, they won't," I said. "They'll just come roll me out of bed in the morning."

Phil just grinned. For an instant he was his great-grandfather, a trooper with Joe Johnston's cavalry, riding out before the Yankee lines just to hear the minié balls slap past his ears.

Down Oak Ridge Road, past the track leading to the First African Baptist, where Phil and I find rough harmony in "Leaning on the Everlasting Arms," down deep in the Oak Ridge woods where we must not go, me cussing and Phil grinning and holding fast to the wheel and past the doe that jumps in front of his truck, then jumps back, and, finally, the blue of the ocean winking though the trees and there we were, deep in forbidden territory.

And there we saw it, the payloaders and bulldozers and dumptrucks skinning off the sand dunes, berming them up into neat one acre squares that might fetch a million bucks apiece. Now we had them. Even here in South Carolina, where half the legislature might misspell environment, you can't mess with the dunes.

Or maybe they had us. There was a burst of profanity and a pickup gave chase.

"Great God Almighty, Phil, I told you!"

"Hold tight, Rog." Phil spun his truck around, ran through the gears like a NASCAR driver, and pretty soon, all we saw behind us was a cloud of dust.

I spent a restless night, waiting for the knock on the door and the squawking radios and the iron around my wrists and the long boatride to the Beaufort County jail where they feed you chicken necks and rice for breakfast and will not turn you loose until you fork over more long green than I could muster.

But instead of that, instead of a summons, three days later, I got a certified letter from the same old slick who had thrown me and Phil the Bug Man off Webb and Oak Ridge. His clients were astounded why anyone would object to the biggest marina on the East Coast. They wanted to sit down for a friendly discussion. Just what was it we wanted, anyway?

So I began a list, short at first. No dredged harbor. No high-density development. No condos. No high-rises. Protect the archaeology with a two hundred acre conservation easement, open to the public. But then the list grew into dreams of all-you-sum-bitches going back to where you came from. Of the quail whistling once more from the huckleberry thickets, of herringbone turtle tracks when the July full moonlight turns the beach bright as day. And of fireflies in the wet woods, talking sweet in codes we cannot begin to understand. Of sweet clean rivers and the oysters safe to eat and creeks full of mullet and the Gullah on the island once again and the watertable rising and the gators back in the swamps where they belong.

Phil and I chewed this over after church, there in the oaken shade, the seawind in the moss and the surf grumbling off in the distance and the lunatic choir of cicadas just taking up their afternoon song, yammering, yammering, like ten thousand door buzzers gone berserk. The preaching had been Baptist, long, and good, all about the Lord lifting you up when you needed it most, and when the sisters busted loose with "Amazing Grace" my hair fairly stood on end.

But church was over and the congregation had shaken hands and gossiped and dwindled until there were just the two of us, speaking of dreams and then more gator nightmares—the spaniel snapped up on a morning walk, the heartbroken owner taken to drink, the kid that somehow managed to outrun one by the Melrose pond, the wardens who came with ropes and snares and went home empty-handed.

And then Phil told me one more. He had not slept well that night, and a little after two, he had broken out his Browning A-5, removed the plug, stuffed it with double ought, duct-taped a flashlight to the barrel and had taken a long walk on Melrose. He had seen no gators, but now he had his gumption back. He would strap on a .357 and he would go after those bass once again.

That's when I added one more item to the list. Phil the Bug Man was going to hunt the Webb Tract next fall. I would make sure of that.

E. O. D.

The river is quiet tonight. The tide has turned and the wind has swapped directions and whispers across the flat slick water, south by south-west, warm and soft and salty, and it smells like a woman in love. Way out in the dark a porpoise breaks and snorts and the moon creeps up over the pines and a whippoorwill calls for a mate that will not come.

Hilton Head, South Carolina, the island where golf is king. I am waiting on a boat, waiting on the end of the dock. E.O.D. Tags on my groceries, the parts for the ailing Toyota, the box of Kentucky sour mash, all bear the initials.

I'm bound for Daufuskie, where the dockhands will paw over a jumble of golf bags and suitcases and sort what is going to the beachfront inn from the groceries and parts and whiskey for people who live on the back of the island like I do. I will collect mine at the end of the dock. E.O.D.

But I am too late for one boat and too early for another, so I pour a dram of Rebel Yell and think about many things, as I do when sipping good whiskey.

I will tell you as much as I can in the time that I have. How I was born to this river, this moon, this porpoise and this lonesome bird, this sucking ebbtide beneath me, this evening like the ones that come to you in dreams. I can tell you about growing up here in glory of sand and wind and rolling surf.

And about running away after I knew pulling up survey stakes would not stop what was going to happen. But that hurts too much, so I will not tell you about that, nor of the women I loved but cut loose, nor of the thirty years it took me to get back to where I started.

Little fish dart in the eddy of the pilings, while Hilton Head stirs behind me like a panther in the dark. Parking lots and BMW's and bars and liquor and women, blonde and already tan, even though it's only April. But I have this great hole in my heart and I got my own good liquor, so I will sit right here and drink it till the boat comes.

The Hilton Head I knew as a child is gone, gone to highways and bridges and blacktop. The wild island ponies, the Gullah rivermen, the old plantations where Yankee swells shot quail and deer and mallards, gone to golf and tennis and million dollar homes where the descendants of slaves have come full circle, pouring tea and whiskey and saying yassuh and yassum all over again.

Hilton Head is gone, but there is still Daufuskie and I am doing what I can to save a little bit of it. "A man gotta stan' for something," Yvonne told me, "An Fuskie the las' place to stand."

Yvonne is fifth generation islander, with a healthy dose of Choctaw on her mother's side. We were on the beach, me carrying a bucket and reeling from the intimations, threats, and rumors; she throwing the net with an ancient and timeless grace. I told her how I wrote the governor and he wrote back and pretty soon I had my own agent's pager number. I told her the phone was clicking and popping and she said "Don' truss em no mo."

So when Bo called from Myrtle Beach we had to be careful what we said. Bo is a writer, too, prominent among those who put me up to all this and maybe the only one who would stand beside me if the bullets start flying, a very real consideration, since we are perceived as standing in the way of sixty million dollars worth of progress.

I asked Bo about his momma and he said she was much better but it's hard to get over a stroke at ninety. Then he asked me about my new project, a screenplay about smuggling.

And I paused and said, "Ah, Bo, we got to assume this phone is not secure."

And he said, "That's OK, cause we ain't doing nothing wrong. We doing battle for the Lord."

"Weren't no condos in the Garden."

He laughed. "Onward Christian Soldiers...." And then he talked like the man on the six o'clock news. "Oh you mean your literary project about something that happened twenty years ago?"

"God bless you, Bo."

"God bless you, too. And goodnight, Mrs. Calabash, wherever you are."

And then there was the conversation with Cindy. Cindy just got her real estate license, but the woman who was going to hire her found out she was friends with me and then there was trouble.

"Why are you guys doing this?"

Bo was back on the island. The painted buntings were working the feeders and the yachts were northbound now.

Bo shrugged and Cindy kept on. "I mean, what's in it for you?"

"The story," Bo said.

Cindy walked in little circles, balled up her fists, and hollered. "Hell, you are creating the story!"

Bo smiled. "And it will be ours when we are done."

Cindy whirled and put a finger in my face. "And you!"

I had been asking myself the same question, so I was ready. "I got four grown kids who love me. I'm gonna leave them a little bit of Daufuskie."

Cindy knew all about the governor and the agent and what not to say on the phone. But we were on my porch and she could speak as she pleased. "Well, what shall we put on your tombstone?"

I had decided there will not be any. Bo knows how to take the ashes and make me part of the rolling surf forever. But the opportunity was too good to let pass.

I looked at Cindy and smiled and she smiled back. She wanted to sell dirt and I wanted to save it, but that did not matter right then.

"E.O.D.," I say.

That was all on the other side of the river. But here I am, stuck on Hilton Head. I pour myself another shot and think of throwing it all into a pile—the files, the maps, the letters from lawyers—and setting it all ablaze. And howling and dancing around it naked and taking my toothbrush and a clean pair of shorts and running south to Eleuthera, the island named for freedom. But I will not do that. I have run before and I do not have another thirty years to get back again.

I will get on the boat and I will cross the slick dark water. I will work on the screenplay and be careful what I say on the phone. I will keep calling the county and the state and the

Feds and I will keep away from the windows at night.

The barnacles pop and the little fish splash when something bigger makes a snatch at them. The ferry comes rattling up the river and the sailboats swing at anchor, masts and spars illuminated, carving the night into fiery zones, with no room for shades of gray.

And I sit on the end of the dock.

E.O.D.

The author gratefully acknowledges
prior publication of the following:

"A Liberal Education," *Sandlapper*
"Dixie Crystals," *The Post and Courier*
"Gatorbait," *Sporting Classics*
"Good Sign" and "Rebel Yell," *Gray's Sporting Journal*
"Off Sinning At the Temple of Sport," *Shooting Sportsman*